EBURY PRESS
LEGENDS OF THE LEPCHAS

A journalist and poet, Yishey Doma has written several books on Sikkim, including *Sikkim: A Hidden Fruitful Valley*, *Faith Healers of Sikkim: Traditions, Legends and Rituals*, and *The Splendour of Sikkim: Cultures and Traditions of the Ethnic Communities*. Her articles on the life and culture in the Sikkim Himalayas have appeared in several newspapers and magazines, as well as in her book *Sikkim: A Travel Companion*. A student of Sikkimese Buddhist philosophy, she has contributed to the award-winning documentary *Lama Dances of Sikkim*, and has also created a book database on the monasteries and temples of Sikkim. Yishey's short story 'Mantras of Love' won the MSN–Random House short-story contest in 2012 and was published in the anthology *She Writes*. She is a recipient of the Sikkim Sahitya Samman, one of Sikkim's top civilian awards, and the first North-east Poetry Award from the Poetry Society (India). She was also one of the first writers-in-residence at the Rashtrapati Bhavan, New Delhi.

Educated at St Edmund's School in Shillong, Pankaj Thapa first began illustrating in his textbooks. After graduating from St Edmund's College, he obtained a master's degree in English at the North-Eastern Hill University, Shillong. He dabbled in journalism for a bit and then settled in Sikkim, where he taught English literature at the Sikkim Government College for thirty-nine years before retiring as associate professor in 2021. He is a founder–member of Green Circle, Sikkim's first environmental group, and a founder–member of Converse, Sikkim's annual literary meet. He has been invited to share his topical cartoons at the Jaipur Literature Festival, Bhutan Literature Festival, Brahmaputra Literature Festival, Tezpur Literature Festival and National Book Trust events. Post retirement, Pankaj Thapa is now a full-time illustrator and graphic designer. His illustration projects include *The Boy Who Had a Dream*, a graphic novel based on a folk tale by Rinpoche Ringu Tulku, Kynpham S. Nongkynrih's *Around the Hearth*, Guru T. Ladakhi's *Monk on a Hill*, Uddipana Goswami's *Where We Come From, Where We Are Going* and Pushpa Sharma's *Nepali Folktales*.

LEGENDS OF THE LEPCHAS

Folk Tales from SIKKIM

YISHEY DOMA

ILLUSTRATIONS BY
PANKAJ THAPA

EBURY
PRESS

An imprint of Penguin Random House

EBURY PRESS

USA | Canada | UK | Ireland | Australia
New Zealand | India | South Africa | China | Singapore

Ebury Press is part of the Penguin Random House group of companies
whose addresses can be found at global.penguinrandomhouse.com

Published by Penguin Random House India Pvt. Ltd
4th Floor, Capital Tower 1, MG Road,
Gurugram 122 002, Haryana, India

First published by Tranquebar,
an imprint of Westland Publications Private Ltd, in 2010
Published in Ebury Press by Penguin Random House India 2023

ISBN 9780143460671

Typeset in Goudy Old Style CGATT
Printed at Gopsons Papers Pvt. Ltd., Noida

www.penguin.co.in

Contents

Children of the Snowy Peaks

𝒥n the beginning, when there was nothing but vast emptiness on earth and in the sky, Itbu-moo, Mother Creator, set out to execute a great plan. She first shaped Kongchen Kongchlo,[1] his wives, Samo Gayzong and Paki Chyu, his brothers, Pawo Hungree and Bagok Chyu, and other mountains or *chyu bee*. As complements to the mountains she created *daa*, the lakes and *roong*, the rivers.

She thought she was done, but something appeared to be missing. She surveyed her handiwork. Why did her creation feel empty? Taking a ball of fresh snow from the summit of Kongchen Kongchlo, Itbu-moo created the first man, Fudongthing,[2] the most-powerful one. Mother

Creator remained unsatisfied. She decided to give Fudongthing, her pet creation, a companion. So she took a bit of *a-yong*[3] from Fudongthing's bones and created the first woman, Nazong Nyu, the ever-fortunate one, as his sister. Later, both became chief deities of the Rongs[4] or Lepchas.

Having created the first man and first woman, brother and sister, Itbu-moo called them and said, 'You are the most beloved of all my creations. I have blessed both of you with supernatural powers. But both of you should live separately as true brother and sister. You can never live together.' Both promised they would follow her decree. She then sent Fudongthing to live on top of a mountain called Nareng-Nangsheng Chyu and Nazong Nyu to Naho-Nathor Daa, a lake located just below the mountain. Itbu-moo also warned them that if they disobeyed her, she would not hesitate to send them down to the foothills to live in the realm of misery.

Fudongthing and Nazong Nyu lived happily enough for some time but one thought began to plague their minds— they were living solitary lives. Nazong Nyu had grown up into a beautiful young woman. She felt life without anyone to share it with was terribly lonely and monotonous. As there was no one else, she thought a lot about Fudongthing, who had grown up into a handsome man. But she remembered Itbu-moo's warning and kept away from him.

Everything was well with their world. As long as Fudongthing and Nazong Nyu behaved in a manner befitting their celestial lineage, they prospered and never suffered any real grief. Their lives in the territory of the Gods were filled with happiness.

But they were not content with happiness alone. And like all humans, they were capable of both good and evil. They soon tired of following the dictates of Mother Creator. Failing to resist temptation, Nazong Nyu constructed a golden ladder and climbed up Nareng-Nangsheng Chyu to meet Fudongthing.

Fudongthing too did not pay heed to Itbu-moo's warning. They began to secretly meet at Tarkol-Partam, a flat piece of meadowland between the mountain and the lake.

One day they decided to meet at Sugyum Sugbling, another lake near Naho-Nathor Daa. Nazong Nyu removed her bangle and kept it near her pillow, as she found it uncomfortable while sleeping. The bangle fell into the lake and from there sprouted *suneol kung*, a mountain palm tree, which later became the abode of Lasso Mung Puno, the demon king.

So absorbed were Fudongthing and Nazong Nyu in their own company that they forgot Itbu-moo and her divine decree and started living together. As a result of this forbidden union, soon a monster-child was born to them. On the birth of the child they remembered Itbu-moo's decree. Both were afraid that Mother Creator would come to know what mischief they had been up to. 'This is an unholy child. We cannot keep him under our roof,' said Fudongthing and threw the child away in the forest. Year after year, a monster-child was born to the couple. And each time they threw the baby away—they would simply leave the babies in cliffs, crags or caves. In this way, seven children were lost.

∾

Many years passed. Itbu-moo came to know that Nazong Nyu had given birth to children but had thrown them away. She wanted to find out how Nazong Nyu was capable of doing such a thing. But no one dared tell her the truth. At last, Ku-hulbu, a dog guarding Nazong Nyu's doorway, spoke up. 'I am Nazong Nyu's doorkeeper and have been guarding her place for many years, O Mother Creator,' the dog said. 'I have seen Fudongthing often meet Nazong Nyu. He is the father of all Nazong Nyu's children.'

Enraged because they had broken their promise to her, Itbu-moo, in a voice as loud as a thunderclap, summoned Fudongthing and Nazong Nyu and pronounced her judgement right away. 'Both of you have disobeyed my orders. You have committed a great sin and have fallen from my grace. I cannot allow you to live in this sacred realm any longer. You will leave immediately and live in the foothills of Kongchen Kongchlo as ordinary humans and suffer for your sins.'

Mortified, Fudongthing and Nazong Nyu left and started living at the foot of Kongchen Kongchlo as husband and wife. Finally, a human child was born to them. Nazong Nyu could not bear to throw away her baby yet again. 'Itbu-moo's curse cannot be washed away,' Nazong Nyu told Fudongthing. 'We are cursed and we have to bear the consequences. This innocent baby has done no evil. Why should this child be punished for our sins? Let us not sin anymore by abandoning this child too.'

And this is how the first Lepcha children were born—Nunglenyu and Kothongfi, the first female and male child, and Numshimnyu and Numbomthing, the second female and male child.

Nazong Nyu while seeing her children grow up realised her past mistakes and turned to Itbu-moo. 'O Mother Creator! O God, giver and keeper of life,' she beseeched her. 'Please forgive us for our past sins. Please come down and bless my family.'

Itbu-moo, who had watched Nazong Nyu labour hard to make her world, understood Nazong Nyu's yearning to get her children blessed. She decided to visit Nazong Nyu's household. Sure that Mother Creator would listen to her prayers, Nazong Nyu began cleaning her house and prepared offerings. And before Itbu-moo arrived, Nazong Nyu hid her first children, Nunglenyu and Kothongfi, inside a cave, for she was embarrassed to present dirty children before Mother Creator.

As expected, Itbu-moo came and blessed the family. Soon

after Mother Creator left, Nazong Nyu called for her children to come out of the cave. But lo! They were not to be found inside the cave. When, eventually, Fudongthing and Nazong Nyu realised their first-born were missing, they began to weep.

Nazong Nyu turned to the benevolence of Itbu-moo again. 'O Mother Creator, we are doomed,' Nazong Nyu cried out. 'We have lost two of our children. Please help us.' Hearing her cries, Mother Creator came down again and enquired about the incident. The couple narrated the entire story. To console them, Itbu-moo showed Nunglenyu and Kothongfi in their spirit form and proclaimed: 'Henceforth, Nunglenyu and Kothongfi will remain as guardian spirits of birth and life of all male and female Lepchas respectively. Besides, they will be the guiding force for the spread of your offspring.' These two deities are still invoked by shamans, especially during Tungbaong Faat or Ingrum Faat,[5] for good health, long life and prosperity of a newborn child.

Everything was well. Numshimnyu and Numbomthing were now brought up as humans in the foothills of the great mountain. However, as the years passed, Fudongthing and Nazong Nyu began to quarrel, often bitterly. Eventually, Fudongthing left and made his palace on the snowy peak seen from Lingthem in Dzongu, the present-day Lepcha reserve in north Sikkim. Nazong Nyu was left alone to manage the earth.

Nazong Nyu lived her life without her companion, but the loss made her very sad. One night, several months after Fudongthing had abandoned her, she made up her mind to go in search of him. Leaving her children behind, she followed Fudongthing's footsteps till she reached the mountain where he had made his abode. The mountain was steep, and Nazong Nyu could not climb it.

But she did not give up. She decided to build a staircase with her necklace to reach the top of the snowy peak to persuade Fudongthing to come back and live with her. As she built each step of the ladder, she sought help from insects like grasshoppers, locusts and daddy longlegs. All these creatures were supposed to be her children. She asked them to hold the ladder firmly as she climbed. The grasshoppers and locusts fled with some of the precious stones. Only daddy longlegs remained to help Nazong Nyu up the ladder. This is why Lepchas believe grasshoppers and locusts die after a few months while daddy longlegs live for a long time, and that their long legs are a result of supporting the staircase for a long time.

On finally reaching the top, Nazong Nyu wept tears of joy for she could see Fudongthing. But to her dismay, Fudongthing ignored her. Nonetheless, she was determined to be near him. So she built her own palace nearby and did not leave his side. The Lepchas believe Fudongthing and Nazong Nyu still live on the mountain facing Lingthem, and every year make offerings to the first man and first woman.

∽

Time flew by. Fudongthing and Nazong Nyu's children grew up and married. They had many children and all of them lived on the foothills of Kongchen Kongchlo in great numbers. They christened their land Mayel Lyang.[6]

Naturally, Itbu-moo was delighted to see the children grow up and prosper. She was particularly delighted to see how they worked at reshaping the world into a pleasant land, giving life to trees and beautiful flowers and planting seeds of different kinds. The prosperity and love in the animal kingdom also caused her much happiness.

Amidst all that plenty and peace, the great Mother Creator, after days of careful deliberation, decided to come to earth and bestow something special on all her creations, including the animals, so that all living beings could live in the world without fearing each other.

'Listen, my children. I am indeed content and pleased to see you so powerful and accomplished. You have done wonders here on earth. You have turned barren lands into a pleasant place of peace and plenty. So happy am I that I want to give one special power to each of you as a gift,' said Itbu-moo. 'But before you ask for that special power, consult among yourselves about your needs. Those of you who have similar needs can form groups and then come together with your wish.'

All the animals and creatures gathered around to discuss what they wanted. Slowly, different groups began to form. Animals like buffaloes, bulls, cows, deer and stag came in a group and asked for a gift which would protect them from others when they were alone. Without uttering a word, Itbu-moo gave them horns. They were very happy and left flaunting their sharp horns.

Next was a group of ferocious-looking creatures—lions, tigers, leopards. Bowing before Itbu-moo, the leader from the group said, 'Great Mother, we would get nowhere without fighting. We would be grateful to you if we can protect ourselves when fighting.' Mother Creator thought for a while and with a wry smile gifted them sharp claws.

As Mother Creator was busy distributing powers to the rather disorderly groups of animals, she sensed one particular creature, a lonely man, standing quietly on one side, patiently waiting his turn while the others jostled to get to the head of the line. Just when Itbu-moo thought she would ask the man what he wanted, a group of birds—vultures, kites, crows—alighted near her and said, 'O Great Mother, we want something that will free us from the creatures of the earth. We think they would be too troublesome to allow us to make a good living.' Itbu-moo smiled and said, 'You are blessed with powerful wings to float and fly in the sky.' The birds instantly took wing and left.

Another group of creatures then took its turn. 'O Mother, the land and the sky are overcrowded. We would be happy to occupy the seas, rivers and oceans,' they pleaded. 'Great Mother, please grant us this gift.' Itbu-moo said, 'You shall have special lungs, fins, tails and some of you will have coats of fur.' At once, the creatures dived into the water and started sporting around happily.

Myriads of her creatures came and Itbu-moo granted all their wishes. It took a long, long time. Finally, when it looked like every one of her creations had been granted its wish, she looked around and saw the man, still standing quietly in the same place. He had not moved or made any demand. This touched her. She signalled him to come closer.

'What would you like to receive?' she asked the man.

The man did not speak. She posed the question again. But still he made no demand. He could not think of anything. Every power had been taken away by those ahead of him.

Touched by the man's generosity towards other beings, Itbu-moo held his hands lovingly, and said, 'I am pleased with you. You showed patience and understanding while there was much disorder among other beings during the distribution of my gifts. For that reason, I would like to personally select a special power for you, the best of the best, far better than what all the other creatures have been given. I will bestow on you such a gift that you will always stand out as superior in comparison. I will bless you with a-yong. And by virtue of this unique asset, you shall lord it over all creatures—on land, sea and sky. You shall till the land, populate the wilderness and govern and be king of all creation.'

Delighted, the man bowed before Mother Creator and returned to his abode in smiles.

True to this blessing, human beings then started building comfortable, cosy and warm dwelling places. They fashioned bows and spears and devised ways and means to tackle the beasts with horns. Those creatures who thought they were free because they had wings to fly high in the sky were also brought down by man's bows and arrows, and pellets. Man made hooks, wove nets and devised rods to capture creatures inhabiting the seas and rivers to eat them as food.

As decreed by the great Itbu-moo, Lepchas believe that humans lord over all other creatures on earth by virtue of that one special gift.

References

1. Kongchen Kongchlo or Mount Khangchendzonga, the third-highest mountain in the world, is regarded by Lepchas as the 'original big stone' and their guardian deity. They believe they have originated from this mountain, which is why a dead body always faces this mountain. As Kongchen Kongchlo was Itbu-moo's first creation, the Lepchas also refer to it as their elder brother. It is also known as Kingtsoom Zaongboo Chyu, the auspicious forehead peak, the highest veil of snow beyond which the spirits of their ancestors dwell in Rum Lyang, the country of the Gods.
2. Also known as Tukbothing.
3. Literally, marrow in the Lepcha language. Here, inference is also to intelligence or wisdom.
4. The Lepchas call themselves Mutanchi Rong Kup Rum Kup, encapsulating the Lepcha story of genesis. It translates as 'Mother's loved ones, children of the snowy peaks, children of God' (Mu is Itbu-moo, Rong is snowy peak, Kup is children and Rum is God). Rong Kup Rum Kup or Rong is the shortened version. The English name, Lepcha, is said to have originated from a Nepali word, lapce or lapca, meaning 'inarticulate speech', which originally had a derogatory connotation.
5. Naming and cleansing ceremony of a newborn baby.
6. Literally, mythical paradise. Also referred to as ancient Sikkim by the Lepchas.

The Death of Lasso Mung Puno

Nunglenyu and Kothongfi were never seen again, but their brother and sister, Numshimnyu and Numbomthing, and their families prospered and grew.

They became the proud parents of many sons and daughters, who begot for them many grandsons and granddaughters. Their descendants spread throughout the land of Mayel Lyang. They built beautiful houses, where all the children lived happily together. Men engaged in hunting and agriculture while women took care of household chores. They never had any misunderstandings and shared work willingly. Unfortunately, this quiet, idyllic life did not remain for long.

Fudongthing and Nazong Nyu's first seven children, who were abandoned and thrown away, had not died. They had grown up to become demons—Rumdu Mung, the devil of small pox; Dom Mung, the devil of leprosy; Arot Mung, the devil of accidents and misfortunes; Ginu Mung, the devil of envy and jealousy; Asor Mung, the devil causing death of unborn children and mothers during childbirth. Others developed into snakes and insects. They all wanted to take revenge on their cruel parents.

The demons and other evil spirits did not want the world of the Lepchas to prosper and started haunting the forests and hills around Mayel Lyang. The eldest among the demons was Lasso Mung. He was also referred to as Lasso Mung Puno or the demon king. He lived in a mountain palm tree on the highest and thickly wooded hill near Talung valley in Dzongu— the present-day Lepcha reserve in north Sikkim.

Angry with his parents for the discrimination, the demon king began to take revenge on Numshimnyu and Numbomthing's children. Seeing the Lepchas live happily in beautiful houses set amid heavenly environs, the demon king was desperate to destroy the Lepcha world. He began to taunt them. 'You sinners,' roared the demon king. 'Come out from your houses and fight me. I don't want you to live so peacefully. I shall destroy you all and rule over Mayel Lyang, just wait and see.'

No one came forward to fight Lasso Mung Puno as Fudongthing and Nazong Nyu's children and grandchildren were meek. They never quarrelled or took up arms. The fact that no one came out to fight him made the demon king very angry, believing that the Lepchas were ignoring his challenge. 'You stupid creatures, why do you hide from me?' the demon king roared. 'Come out in the open and fight.' The Lepchas remained inside their homes. 'You cowards,' taunted the demon king, 'you have no right to live. If you cannot come out and fight, it is better you turn into rats and live in holes like them.'

Now the Lepcha men were truly provoked by the demon king's scorn and insolence. They decided to take up the challenge and came out of their houses. A savage and tumultuous battle ensued between the Lepcha men and the demons. The battle continued for many days. Days became weeks. Weeks became months. Months became years. Many people were wounded and many died.

Lasso Mung Puno, whose thirst for vengeance had not been quenched, was enraged further on seeing many Lepchas survive. 'I will teach you humans the lesson of your lives! This time, I will finish your world,' he warned, and using his demonic powers transformed himself into different forms—ox, tiger, dragon, snake, horse, sheep, monkey, dog and pig. The men were dumbfounded, and some of them grew apprehensive, for it seemed to them that Lasso Mung Puno had mysterious powers and would never die. How terrified they were to fight against something that had the power to change itself into various forms! How many different forms of animals and birds could this demon transform into? The Lepchas continued to fight these manifestations, but soon they sensed defeat and fled the battlefield, taking shelter in the forest and caves up in the mountains. As they fled, the demons took over Mayel Lyang.

The Lepchas remained in hiding. They may have found a place safe from the demon king, but they suffered tremendously in the forests. They had nothing to eat and roamed about hunting for some animals or looking for food such as tubers or yams that could satisfy their hunger. It was during these forays into the forest that the Lepcha men discovered many plants, thus earning the tag of 'gentle botanists'. But they had only one thought on their minds: how to end their misery for good.

The demons had become all-powerful. The Lepcha warriors were thoroughly demoralised. Bothered by the ongoing trouble in Mayel Lyang, some of the gods in Rum Lyang wondered who would be the strongest man among the humans to kill the demon king, but they could not find anyone. The Lepchas had no alternative but to pray and seek help from Itbu-moo to save them from the demon king.

'O Mother Creator! Please help us,' the Lepcha warriors entreated. 'The demons have been torturing us for a long time. We don't have a proper home to call our own as we have been moving from one place to another, running away from the demons. Save us from these demons, O Mother.'

Itbu-moo, who saw everything and understood that Lasso Mung Puno's design was to wipe out the human race from these beautiful mountains, sent a bamboo species (*payong*) to rescue the people and also to act as a mediator between Rum Lyang and Mayel Lyang. Unfortunately, the bamboo reached only a height on the mountain and stayed rooted there.[1] Next, Mother Creator sent a beetle that neglected its work and merely planted another bamboo, which too failed to help the suffering Lepchas. Yet another beetle was sent but it transformed itself into another bamboo species. With bamboos in plenty, the Lepchas began to learn how to use the plant, including making handicrafts and using it when making offerings to the gods, and this is followed even today. A grasshopper was sent next, followed by a cricket but all failed to carry out the errand which Mother Creator had entrusted them with.

As a last resort, on top of Pandim Chyu or Mount Pandim, the Great Mother created a *bongthing*,[2] a powerful shaman. 'You are very dear to me, as are the Lepchas,' she said. 'I will bless you with supernatural powers. You will have to go to earth and destroy all the demons to save the Lepcha people. And after you gain victory over the demons, you will act as mediator between Rum Lyang and Mayel Lyang.'

'What would be the best thing, O good Mother, to take with me to Mayel Lyang if I am to win against the demons?' asked the bongthing. Itbu-moo gave him the gifts of ginger, garlic and a tree whose fruits produced light when ignited—items used by bongthings during rituals even to this day.

The bongthing reached Mayel Lyang. Standing on top of a mountain near Tharkaol Tam-e-Tam or the valley of deliverance, he started laughing loudly. His laughter was so loud that it shook the earth and echoed in the mountains, waking Lasso Mung Puno from his deep slumber.

'This is no usual sound. Mother Creator has heard our prayers!' the Lepcha people thought and peeped out of their hiding places to see who their saviour was. The bongthing spotted the Lepchas and knew that they had lost their morale in their fight against the demons. 'I must do something for this terrified lot,' he said to himself. At the same time, he was apprehensive that with the demons having spread all over Mayel Lyang, it had become difficult to fight them.

Lasso Mung Puno, bothered by the great laughter of so unique a being, could do nothing other than send a retinue of demons to find out who the mischief-maker was. When the demons saw the bongthing, they were scared. Without asking him anything, they rushed back to their king, and said, 'O Lord! We have seen a very powerful man today. As he laughs and opens his mouth, the whole earth shakes. We were so scared that we didn't even go near him.'

'You fools!' shouted the demon king. 'Get lost, you good-for-nothing scoundrels! How dare you come here with that news? Go away and don't ever show your faces. It was my mistake that I trusted you.'

What a shame, thought Lasso Mung Puno. What a horrible disgrace! His demons had not even been able to approach the man.

He summoned his chief minister. 'Go immediately, minister,

go up there and find out who this man is. If he acts smart, tear him to pieces,' ordered the demon king. 'I will not leave these humans. I will crush them.'

The faithful chief minister went to the foothill of the mountain and facing the giant man said, 'Hello, who are you? Tell me, why have you come here? My master Lasso Mung Puno has sent me here to ask about you and if need be, to kill you.'

The giant man gave another loud laugh and answered, 'I am a bongthing with supernatural powers and dear to Itbumoo. I have been sent by her to kill Lasso Mung Puno, your so-called king, and to save the Lepcha people from the clutches of the demons. Tell your master that if he wants to stay alive he should stop torturing the humans and leave Mayel Lyang right away.'

Terrified, the chief minister went to Lasso Mung Puno and reported the whole incident. The demon king was furious. 'Who does he think he is? Who was he laughing at? Himself? Does he not know I am the king of Mayel Lyang? How can he challenge me? If he wants to fight, I am ready for it.'

The demon king was in a terrible rage. At once he summoned all his demon forces and set out to fight the bongthing. On seeing the crowd of demons ready to wage war against him, the bongthing laughed, loud. The earth cracked, reverberated, scaring the demon army away. But Lasso Mung Puno was least bothered. 'Do you think your laughter will scare me away? You are wrong. I will kill you! I will kill everybody and I will continue to rule over Mayel Lyang!' he roared.

No sooner had he said this, the demon king sent a shower of arrows upon the shaman. Equally powerful, the bongthing warded the arrows off. In return, he sent thousands of arrows, killing many demons. This continued for a long time. Some of the demons thought of giving up the fight. But Lasso Mung Puno was determined to destroy the bongthing.

The demon king transformed himself into a tiger and attacked the bongthing. The bongthing used his sword, wounding the tiger. Lasso Mung turned into a horse but came under the bongthing's divine spear.

Still the demon king refused to accept defeat and the fight continued for several days. Hoping against hope, the shaman thought of using his final power. He took out an arrow with *nyung pak* or poison and said, 'You will not survive if I use this.' As the poisonous arrow pierced his forehead, Lasso Mung Puno took the form of a monstrous mountain eagle and flew away in extreme pain. Seeing their leader fly away, the rest of the demon forces panicked and fled to the depths of the world.

On hearing that the demons had fled, all the Lepcha men and women came out from their hiding places and joined the bongthing. The demon king, however, continued to wreak havoc on the humans and kill children. The Lepchas and the bongthing knew they had to find and destroy the demon who had taken the form of an eagle. They searched under rocks, in forests, lakes and caves but could not find the eagle. At last they discovered him atop the mountain palm tree in Talung valley.

The Lepchas, the bongthing and even the Gods got together and planned to cut down the tree. But what they managed to chop of the tree during the day, would grow again overnight. The men chopped for days, but no amount of chopping destroyed the tree.

Finally three gods—Komyothing, Komsithing and Saktsumthing—with the help of the Lepcha men and the bongthing began to look for an appropriate volunteer. They found one in the form of pushikbu, a kind of caterpillar that constantly eats away at wood, day and night, without being seen.

The plan was successful. The pushikbu gnawed away at the tree till it became hollow and fell down, forcing Lasso Mung

Puno to fly down to the villages of Dzongu at Sakyong. The remains of this tree, it is said, can be seen as a big opening at the foot of the Talung mountains, also called Sanyol mountains. Water gushing out of it is the source of the river Rangyong, flowing through the heart of Dzongu.

At Sakyong, the demon king took shelter in another tree, the *sangli kung*, which was crushed by the demon's weight. Then it flew towards Pentong, Laven, Tingbong, Lungdeum Adong, Lingthem and Liklyang, killing and eating humans who came in his way, with the three Gods and the Lepcha warriors in hot pursuit. All these villages got their names after Lasso Mung Puno flew over them.

At last the Lepcha warriors reached Lasso Chungrong or the grave of Lasso Mung near a spring in present-day Phamrong waterfalls in west Sikkim. Near this spring, the warriors came upon a bird called kugreafo. On the advice of this bird, the warriors made a cage near the spring and plastered it with *yak-san*, a strong sticky substance.

Then the bird started to annoy Lasso Mung Puno by calling out to him constantly whenever the demon eagle came out to drink water at the spring. When the demon bird attacked the kugreafo in anger, its claws got stuck in the cage. The warriors seized the opportunity and killed the demon king. The kugreafo was later adorned with *kazi-kasu pok*, the white crown-like feathers on its head.

In order to get rid of the menace of the demons, the bongthing summoned all the other demons and evil spirits, who had fled to the depths of the world, for a meeting. In this meeting, the bongthing agreed to offer animal and bird sacrifices to the demons, who in return promised to leave Mayel Lyang for the Lepchas and to stop bothering them.

To ensure the demons would keep the covenant, the bongthing asked them to swear by spitting on a rock. The oath turned out to be so strong that it shattered the rock to pieces. When repeating the act in a lake, the water in the lake dried up.

But as the days passed, it became clear the demons did not plan to keep to their promise. The bongthing had to then spend a lot of time appeasing them and could not pay attention to his responsibility as the mediator between Rum Lyang and Mayel Lyang for the welfare of humans. He then chose Nyolik Nyosong, a female from among the human beings, and made her a *mun*, a powerful Lepcha female shaman. With due ceremony he delegated the responsibility of the welfare of the Lepchas to her. In this ceremony, the powerful bongthing used three blades of elephant grass to transmit his heaven-given divinity to the mun—which is why this grass still plays an important role in rituals conducted by the muns.

This episode marked the origination of muns among the Lepchas. It is the mun-bongthing who offers prayers and sacrifices to the Gods on behalf of the Lepchas, especially when someone falls sick or is considered to be inflicted by the demons. In due course of time, the muns also became responsible for performing the Sanglyon ceremony, a ceremony of taking the souls of the dead back to Rum Lyang.

In those ancient times, the Lepchas of Mayel Lyang did not know many rites and rituals. They prayed to Itbu-moo morning and night. Although they knew about evil spirits and demons and were afraid to go anywhere near them, they did not think it necessary to make offerings to appease them. It was the bongthing, a man of great wisdom and understanding of the mysteries of life, who started making sacrifices to the chief of the spirits. And it is from him the Lepchas learnt to propitiate and pay obeisance to more than one supreme creator. However, it is said, the powerful bongthing could not appease Dom Mung, the evil spirit of leprosy, as it had not come to the meeting the bongthing had called. That is why the Lepchas believe that leprosy is incurable.

∾

The Lepcha warriors remained suspicious that Lasso Mung Puno had not died. Thoughts of the demon king's power to change forms began to bother them. Even as the demon's body lay like a lifeless log, neither moving nor rotting, they felt Lasso Mung Puno would rise using his demonic powers and attack them again. Everybody grew apprehensive.

One brave Lepcha warrior decided to go up to the body and check whether the demon king was alive or dead. Armed with a sword, ready to strike the demon should he stir, he placed his hand on Lasso Mung Puno's breast. 'His heart is still pumping and his body is warm!' yelped the warrior. Terrified, the Lepcha took to his heels. 'Lasso Mung Puno is still alive! Lasso Mung Puno is not dead! He is unconscious. I could feel his heart pumping. He will soon regain consciousness and resume fighting. Let us do something.'

But the demon king did not get up for a long time. Ever fearful that Lasso Mung Puno would awaken, the Lepchas sent another brave man to go and gouge out the demon's eyes. If the demon king ever got up, he would not be able to confront them since he would now be blind, the Lepchas thought.

Cautiously approaching the body, the Lepcha warrior who had been chosen for the mission, took out his dagger and pierced both eyes. Blood oozed out. But the body remained warm and the heart continued to beat. The warrior was now scared the demon would get up because of the pain in its eyes, and ran away.

Still the demon did not get up. This time the Lepchas thought it would be better to cut the limbs and the body into many small pieces. The demon king would then not be able to get up. Slinging a *bhamphok*³ on his waist attached with a rope, a Lepcha warrior was despatched to cut up the demon. This man too found the body of the demon warm, his heart pounding, his eyes pierced. He thought the demon with his magical powers would come back to life and kill them. So he took out his sword and cut off the demon's limbs and neck. Blood oozing from his eyes and wounds, the demon lay in a pool of blood.

The warrior thought, 'Who knows, with his magical powers, the separated parts of the body may join. It is certainly better if these are crushed into tiny pieces and thrown in the air.' So he called some more Lepcha warriors and together they hacked the demon's flesh into pieces, broke all the bones and the head and threw all these up in the air, like dust particles. Now they were sure the demon could not harm them anymore.

The demon had been vanquished. The Lepchas celebrated for seven long days. The bongthing decided to honour all those who had fought bravely by giving them titles in accordance with their merit.

He gave the highest honour, the title of Lutsaommoo, to the one who had gone first to see whether the demon king was dead.

The men who had prayed to Itbu-moo and requested her to deliver the Lepchas from the clutches of the demons were given the title of Munlaommoo.

The brave man who had pierced Lasso Mung Puno's eyes was given the title Seemickmoo.

The Lepcha who broke the body of the demon king was given the title Sungootmoo, while those who had helped crush the body into tiny pieces and scatter it in the air were honoured with the title Sungdyangmoo.

Not only were these brave soldiers awarded but also those

who had made arms for battle. The bongthing gave the title of Karvomoo to those who had made the weapons.

Those who provided food during the war were given the title Joriboo.

Those Lepchas who had served the bongthing and Nyolik Nyosong mun during the battle were given the title Adenmoo, while those men who had helped to make bows and arrows to fight Lasso Mung Puno were given the title Phyoong Talimmoo.

Those who helped in constructing bridges and roads and making ropes and bow-strings were given the title Brimoo.

These ten titles are the patrilineal clans of the Lepchas. These ten different clans are also called Rong Kup Kati or Rong Kati, which means ten Lepchas, while the laws and regulations for them are called Rong Kati Tyum.

It took twelve years for the Lepchas to kill Lasso Mung Puno. Because of the long war and suffering, people learnt the concept of time, dates, months and years and also learnt to use different forms of wild food and plants as medicines and many other things for survival. Lasso Mung Puno was killed on the last day, Marlavo, of the twelfth month of the Lepcha calendar. Marlavo marks the end of the year, and the very next day is Kurnyet Nyom Chot Kat, the first day of the first month of the New Year, also called Nambun or Namsoong.

To commemorate the victory, Marlavo Tyangrigong Sonap, or victory over evil, is celebrated every year on Nambun.

∞

Lasso Mung Puno continues to torment the Lepchas. He was a supernatural creature and it was impossible for the Lepcha warriors to kill him. The demon remained alive in spirit. He was unwilling to surrender and was determined to take revenge against the humans. The demon king was so powerful that the powdered flesh of his body turned into blood-sucking parasites like bugs, mosquitoes, lice and fleas; his crushed bones became wasps, scorpions, snakes and other poisonous insects; while his blood gave birth to leeches—all which still continue to plague humans.

References

1. This particular bamboo, payong (hollow bamboo), is usually seen thriving on high mountains. Lepchas weave their traditional hat (*sumo thakdip*) from this bamboo.
2. Bongthing means the original and respected one. It is derived from two words: *abong*, meaning original or main, and *athing*, meaning honourable or respected. The word also corresponds to a Lepcha shaman.
3. A weapon for self-defence used by the Lepchas; now also functions as a multipurpose knife.

The Crown of Music

After the killing of Lasso Mung Puno, the Lepchas regained their morale. There was much rejoicing among the men and women. To celebrate, they prepared a huge dancing ground and sent word to all, announcing the beginning of a new life. Everyone was welcome to join in to celebrate freedom and the triumph of good over evil.

Young and old, musicians, singers and dancers from across Mayel Lyang converged upon the celebration ground. They enjoyed the festivities as only those who have lived for long with so much suffering and devoid of happiness can. As the sound of their laughter, coupled with the music, echoed throughout earth, the God of music and dance, Narok Rum, descended from Rum Lyang with his divine entourage.

The Lepchas danced day and night. Men shunned their work and women ignored their household chores, submerging themselves in the dancing. Intrigued by their rhapsody and total involvement, Narok Rum and his entourage could do nothing but quietly join in. No one recognised the God of music—the one they revered—who was in their midst.

However, all eyes were on Narok Rum's *chat*, a crown made of the feathers of the nambong punnong, a racket-tailed drongo, considered the king of birds because of its long tail. Narok Rum's charming personality, the colourful crown on his head and his majestic dance steps mesmerised the Lepcha men and women. They followed the heavenly dancer all around the dancing ground.

They danced for seven days. On the last day, the procession moved to another village. The people of this village also came forward and joined the procession. Narok Rum was very happy to see everyone celebrating in their own carefree style. When the celebrations ended, the God of music wanted to give the dancers something as a token of his appreciation.

Narok Rum called the leader of the dancers and congratulated him on the wonderful dancing. 'Well done, all you music and dance lovers!' said the heavenly being. 'I am Narok Rum, the God of music. Your dancing was magnificent! I am very pleased. Ask me a wish and I shall grant it right away.'

When the leader heard that their visitor was none other than the God of music himself, he was speechless. The women who had danced with Narok Rum turned red with embarrassment. 'Narok Rum! Narok Rum was in our midst!' whispered the Lepchas.

Unnerved, all the Lepchas could do was simply gaze at

Narok Rum's crown. It was long and beautiful. Other men in his entourage had similar crowns decorated with yellow, blue, black and red plumes and tails of birds like the sa-himfo or the ashy drongo.

'Lord of music, we would love to have some of the beautiful feathers that decorate your crown,' uttered the leader of the dancers, who like the others seemed awestruck by the crown. The God of celestial music seemed taken aback by this request but finding all the men and women staring at his crown in silence, concluded they must really like it.

'Come and take this crown of music from me,' Narok Rum told the leader. Placing the chat on his head, the God of music blessed him with these words: 'From today onwards, all of you present here will excel in singing and dancing and everyone will like your performances. May you all cherish the gift of music and dance forever. May you all become absolute masters of Lepcha folk songs, dances, music and musical instruments. And when I feel like it, I too will descend to Mayel Lyang and dance with you.' With these words, Narok Rum vanished as swift as an arrow. His entourage presented their respective crowns to the others and followed him.

From that day on, when dancing, the Lepchas wear feather crowns as proudly as royals wear their jewel-encrusted ones. It is also said that those who are blessed with a good voice and graceful movements are those who have received Narok Rum's blessings. They are considered to be his favourites.

To this day, the Lepchas celebrate for seven days. On the eve of Nambun, they make an effigy of the demon king, Lasso Mung Puno. They use cereals, small twigs and leaves, all the things which Lasso Mung Puno had used when hiding, before he was killed. The Lepcha men strike the effigy with spears, swords and sticks, enacting a mock battle with the demon. Shouts of 'Victory of Mother Creator, defeat of the demon king' ring the air as they take out the effigy in a procession, eventually setting it on fire. Then the Lepchas offer prayers to Itbu-moo.

This marks the beginning of the seven days of dancing and singing songs in praise of Narok Rum.

Narok Rum Ma, Rong Dung Gil Sa Vum Ik Bu Lo
Ae . . . Ae . . . Narok Rum Adom Sawoh Topsit Tucheot Ka
(Narok Rum, the creator of Lepcha music
Now is the time to praise you)

High up in Rum Lyang, the God of music hears the songs and blesses the Lepchas.

The Marriage of Tarbong Nom and Narip Nom

In the days of yore, when men and animals lived together in peace and spoke the same language, there lived a handsome and robust hunter known as Tarbong Nom. He lived in a small village in the foothills of Mount Khangchendzonga. Like all men in the hamlet, he was very fond of hunting and fishing, which he engaged in whenever the opportunity presented itself.

One winter morning, Tarbong's mother wanted him to go and hunt for some venison. 'Son, come back soon but don't come back empty-handed,' said his mother. Tarbong went striding off in the direction of Pari Pagyen with his bow and arrow. His mother had packed enough food to last him at least three months in the forest.

Tarbong roamed the forests of Pari Pagyen in search of deer. His rations slowly began to run out. 'How can I fulfil my mother's wish for venison?' he wondered. Neither the village elders nor his mother had told him that deer never venture where humans have trodden, at least for three months. When his food was nearly finished, Tarbong had no choice but to leave the forest.

After days of searching for food, he arrived at the top of a mountain, Paki Chyu, tired and exhausted, and looked for shelter for the night. Not finding a comfortable spot to set up camp there, he climbed up Palyang Chyu. Standing on top of this mountain, the young hunter, to his surprise, could see a tree laden with fruit with hundreds of birds perched on its branches. 'This is a beautiful tree. I must go there,' he thought. As all humans are, Tarbong was greedy to capture the colourful birds that had filled him with delight.

There was no village in sight when Tarbong reached the tree. He decided to spend the night under the tree. His long trek through the forest had made him very hungry. He sat under the tree and took out his last packet containing stale slices of buckwheat bread. He ate the bread in silence, enjoying every bite immensely, with thoughts of catching all the birds on the tree for his mother. When he had finished eating, he made a bamboo trap to catch the birds roosting above him, a technique his mother had taught him when he was merely a toddler. Tarbong managed to catch a few of them. He started for home very early next morning as he wanted to reach home before it was dark.

When Tarbong reached home, he found his mother eagerly anticipating his arrival. 'Why are you so late, my son? What have you been doing all these months?' asked his mother anxiously.

'The world outside is so beautiful, Mother,' answered Tarbong. 'I saw countless birds on a fruit tree on a mountain. Here are some of them. If they are good, accept them as gifts for the food you give me every day and if you don't like them, you can throw them away.'

'Son, thank you. These are good to eat. I accept them as recompense for the food I had given you during your days in the forest,' replied his mother, happy that her son was appreciative of her efforts to take care of him.

The next morning, Tarbong, mesmerised by the memory of the fruit tree, again set out in the same direction even though his mother advised him not to venture out. He bade her goodbye and set forth towards his destination. As he walked the path, he thought of all those colourful birds. He was also bothered by his inability to get venison for his mother despite spending several months in the forest. His feet seemed to know the way, even though his mind was preoccupied, and he made good time towards his destination.

On reaching, Tarbong set the traps again and went to look for a village, thinking he might need to spend a few nights. To his horror, on returning to his shelter under the tree in the afternoon, Tarbong discovered only twigs and leaves hanging on his traps instead of the birds. His world came crashing down. 'Someone must have played a trick on me,' he thought. Puzzled and curious to know who the prankster was, he set up some more snares and hid behind a rock. Late in the afternoon, he saw a beautiful girl coming through the woods, freeing the birds from the traps and replacing them with twigs and leaves. Could she be a fairy from Rum Lyang, wondered Tarbong, quickly falling in love with her.

Tarbong sneaked up and grasped the girl from behind. The girl jumped, looking at him in amazement. His own heart pounding, Tarbong asked, 'Why did you free the birds from the trap?'

'I am the guardian and protector of these birds. The birds have an equal right to live in Mayel Lyang as we do,' replied the girl.

On Tarbong's persistent request to know more about her, she continued, 'I am Narip Nom and I come from Sakyong. If you really want my hand in marriage, you must ask my mother and my uncle.'

Feeling confident that Narip Nom would not run away, Tarbong loosened his grip on the girl. As soon as he did so, she ran away deep into the forest. Tarbong ran after her, but found himself falling behind. He shouted after her, 'Will I see you again? I would like to take you to my mother and present you as my gift in place of the deer she had asked for.'

'Sure, you will, provided you follow what has to be done,' came the reply.

Dejected, but determined to win his love, Tarbong returned home. Day by day, he grew more miserable. He stopped going to hunt. When his mother could not bear her son's sadness any longer, she asked him what the matter was. On hearing his tale, she advised him to go to his older brother, Kumsheything, who lived in another village.

Kumsheything heard his brother's story and saw the lovelorn state he was in. 'Well, brother, you will have to pay for it. You will have to win over Narip Nom's mother and her uncle and seek their approval for marriage. This is not as easy a task as you think. To please them, you need to collect different kinds of gifts. You will also need to offer Sakyu Rum Faat[1] to the Gods with *chee*[2] and butter. Do you love her enough to do that?' asked Kumsheything.

'I love Narip Nom more than anything in this world. I will do anything to get her hand. Just tell me what I need to do,' replied Tarbong.

Kumsheything was very pleased with the reassurance that his brother could do anything to get his love. He called a village meeting to finalise the marriage plans and acquire the items to be presented as the bride's price. Kumsheything, being one of the elders in the village, told his brother, 'Brother Tarbong, you have to go to Nepal and get a pig and *tandyo fyu*, the thick hand-shaped earthen pot, from there, as you need to present these items to the bride's family.'

Tarbong went to Nepal and brought back these items. Then he was asked to go to Bhutan to get *kamo*, a beautiful material out of which a *dum-dyam* was made for the girl's mother. Presents for Narip Nom's siblings and uncle were also bought. Tarbong was sent to Tibet to get a woollen rug, *mongbree*[3] seeds from Mayel valley and a bull from Kamyong valley.

Everything was now ready except the chee. Kumsheything said, 'We now need to make a fire to cook the mongbree seeds to make chee.'

Alas! The world was without fire because it was in the possession of Deut Mung, the devil hiding in Mashyok Matel, a place between heaven and earth. They all knew it was very difficult to fight him to bring back fire.

'O dear brother, we are all afraid of Deut Mung. There are so many demons in that place and I am so meek they will eat me if I go there. But if I don't, my dream of making Narip Nom my bride will be lost forever,' said Tarbong dejectedly.

What was Kumsheything to do? What a shame if he was not able to help his beloved brother. He turned to his village and all the creatures in Mayel Lyang, pleading with them to help him get just enough fire to boil the mongbree seeds to make chee.

Ka-rhyakfo, a black-backed kaleej pheasant, on hearing Kumsheything's plea for help offered to fly to the demon's house and steal the fire. In no time the bird reached Deut Mung's abode. It was a lonely spot. The bird looked for the fire. He found it quickly as no one was there and clasping it in his beak flew back to the village.

But after having flown several miles, the bird felt hungry and laying the fire on a branch of a chestnut tree, ventured out in search of some food. Suddenly, a strong wind blew and the tree caught fire, spreading to other trees. A great fire then raged in the forest. The poor bird got caught in the fire, and as a result has short feathers and peeled-off reddish skin around its eyes.

When several days had passed without the bird's return, and Kumsheything was just about to give up hope, a grasshopper volunteered to bring back the fire. This small insect was no ordinary creature; it had divine powers. When he reached Deut Mung's abode, only silence greeted him. The devil was not there. Seizing the opportunity, this tiny creature leaned against the fireplace and using its divine powers turned the devil's abode upside down.

When the devil returned, he was very angry on seeing his house in shambles. Who had dared do this to his house? Just then, he felt an insect on his back. He tried to catch it, but the insect was too tiny for the devil's hands and hopped away. This only fuelled Deut Mung's anger. 'You tiny fellow, how dare you destroy my house like this,' he threatened. 'I will kill you.'

'Well, if you kill me, who will change your house back to its original order?' answered the grasshopper.

This made Deut Mung pause and think. 'So then, tell me, how can I help you so that you set my house in order again?' asked Deut Mung.

'Kumsheything has sent me to get some fire from you. If you part with a bit of fire, I will rearrange your house,' replied the grasshopper.

Concerned that he would never see the beautiful abode he was so proud of in its proper order, Deut Mung agreed to the deal. Soon the devil's house was back to its original form and the grasshopper got a bit of fire. Happy to see his house again the way he liked it, the devil even gave the grasshopper tips on how to make fire with flint and tinder. He also advised the grasshopper not to carry the fire in his mouth.

But the grasshopper was so pleased with his own efforts that he did not pay heed to the devil's advice and clasped the fire in his mouth. The fire he was carrying in his mouth burnt out. When he reached back, he had no fire to give Kumsheything. Fortunately, he had paid attention when the devil had taught him how to make fire from flint and tinder, and he passed this on to the villagers.

At last, Tarbong's people could boil the mongbree seeds. But there was another problem. There was no *buth*, a powder which ferments the boiled mongbree seeds into chee.

The Lepchas knew they could not go to ask for Narip Nom's hand in marriage without the chee. The Lepchas were a shy people and drinking chee roused the spirit of gaiety, humour and liveliness in them. How would the shy Lepchas impress Narip Nom and her village without drinking chee? What was a wedding without merriment?

Buth was only available from Anyu Matli Mu,[4] the God of wine, who lived in Tongdek Mardek, the netherworld, far, far below Deut Mung's world. Tongdek Mardek, legend says, is neither hell nor a dark place but just a bit unapproachable. Living there, Anyu Matli Mu also creates earthquakes, which the Lepchas believe is a sign of her anger. Kumsheything convened another meeting of all the animals, birds and humans of Mayel Lyang to find a volunteer who would have the courage and wisdom to bring some buth from the netherworld.

A tambum,[5] proud of his power to fly, said, 'Listen to me, my friends. I will take up this responsibility for I can fly as well as dig into holes. I will go to the underworld to fetch the buth and bring it to you. You can reward me when I return.'

The bumblebee, after many adventures, succeeded in reaching Tongdek Mardek.

After staying with Anyu Matli Mu for some time, the bumblebee succeeded in bringing up the matter of the buth. To his delight, she gave it to him immediately and he joyfully brought it back to the Lepchas. Everybody was happy, till they discovered that what the bumblebee had brought from the underworld was not the real buth. Anyu Matli Mu had been too clever for the poor creature; he had been tricked.

Humiliated to the core, the bumblebee flew back home. On the way he received a message from the queen of flowers forbidding him to show his face in her flower kingdom. He was the queen's favourite attendant. Why was she so upset with him that she had banished him from her kingdom? He found out that it was none other than a *pago reep*,[6] the queen's other attendant, who had complained to the queen about the tambum having left some of the fake buth in the queen's chambers. This made the bumblebee wild, and a once gentle, harmless creature now developed a sting and started attacking anyone who came in its way.

Seeing the bumblebee's deadly rage, the pago reep thought: 'I have to do something or else the tambum will eat me up. He will take revenge on me.' When a furious tambum landed on the pago reep, she closed her petals, killing the tambum. Whenever a tambum landed on a pago reep, the petals would close, killing the tambum. Several tambums lost their lives. When the other tambums found their friends missing, they went in search of them and found them trapped inside the pago reeps.

Some of the senior tambums prayed to Itbu-moo. Their prayers were heard. Mother Creator came down to Mayel Lyang and asked the bumblebees, 'Beautiful little beings, what has made you suffer so much that you have invoked my name?'

'O Mother, we are in a grave situation. We have nothing to eat and as we go in search of nectar, the pago reeps close their petals and kill us. Please liberate us, your children, from the clutches of the death trap,' pleaded the tambums, shedding tears.

Itbu-moo summoned the leader of the pago reeps. 'Is it true that you are being cruel to these bumblebees? Since you have been killing them, you will flower only at midnight and your petals will fade away before sunrise,' said Mother Creator, and thus proclaiming, disappeared.

Now the pago reeps were very unhappy. No birds or insects came to sit on them or sang songs near them since the flowers faded away early in the morning.

Itbu-moo could see one of her own creations suffering. She descended to earth once more and asked the pago reeps, 'Why are you so sad? Everyone else is happy in Mayel Lyang. The rivers dance merrily down to the plains. The animals and birds sing as they go about their lives. My gentle and sober children, the Rongs, worship nature and speak a sacred language. Why are you the only unhappy ones?'

'We have become disfigured. We have no beauty. In this sacred land of Mayel Lyang, we are alone. No one comes near us. We have lost our very existence. There is no reason for us to live any longer,' said the pago reeps.

Itbu-moo listened carefully and said, 'I am sorry to hear your sad plight but I cannot withdraw the blessings that I gave the tambums nor can I take back the curse I put on you. Nevertheless, I shall try to relieve your sadness.'

Calling all the pago reeps near her, Mother Creator blessed them. 'Your petals will fade away before dawn. However, henceforth, your seeds will look like flowers and they will remain unpolluted, completely pure and clean. My beloved children, the Rongs, will use your seeds as sacred flowers in all festivals and ceremonies. You will be offered at the feet of the gods and will be used as garlands. The Rongs will worship you as they do Kongchen Kongchlo.'

Before leaving earth, Itbu-moo also called the tambums to

her side and said, 'I have blessed the pago reeps. Now you too will be blessed. Your dead friends cannot be brought back to life. However, those dead friends of yours will live in Mayel Lyang in the form of *chimbu-suguk-bur*.'[7] And so the tambums never collect nectar from this plant because they know it is their dear friends.

Kumsheything and Tarbong still needed the buth. Who would now be brave enough to go to Tongdek Mardek again? This time the humble tangder[8] offered.

When he reached Anyu Matli Mu's abode, he found she was an old woman. He hit upon the plan of pretending to be her grandson, and striking up an amicable conversation with her, soon started living in her house. He thought by being there day and night he would, one day, see her making chee and where she hid the buth.

But Anyu Matli Mu was very clever. She would begin the process of making the brew only after sending the cockroach out on an errand or when he fell asleep. Many days passed and the cockroach grew bored.

One day, the old woman started preparing chee when the cockroach was at home. He pretended not to notice. But when the time came for mixing the buth, Anyu Matli Mu brought a closely-woven basket and covered the tangder with it so that he could no longer see what she was doing.

Trapped under the basket, the tangder sat quietly for a while. It wasn't long before an idea struck him. He remembered seeing a wide-meshed basket in one corner of the brewing room. 'O Anyu,' cried out the cockroach, 'I can see my mother going towards the cowshed with my little brother.'

Hearing this, Anyu Matli Mu stopped what she was doing and called back, 'How can you see from behind the close weaves of the basket?'

'I can see that you are facing the basket and talking to me,' the cockroach answered.

'Tell me, my grandson, how can I cover you up completely so that you can't see anything?' asked Anyu Matli Mu.

'Grandma, please, cover me with anything, but do not cover me with the other basket in the room. It will suffocate me,' the tangder answered.

No sooner had she heard these words, the woman replaced the close-weaved basket with the wide-meshed basket over the cockroach. Confident the cockroach could not see her now, Anyu Matli Mu continued with preparing the brew. That was exactly what the cockroach had wanted. Through the big gaps in the weave of the basket, he watched Anyu Matli Mu take the buth from a tiny gourd container slung around her neck. It had been concealed under her plaited hair all this time! Pouring it into her palm, she crushed it into a powder and sprinkled it over the boiled mongbree.

As soon as she replaced the tiny container around her neck, Anyu Matli Mu removed the basket that was covering the cockroach and said, 'Little fellow, you can see how I prepare chee.' She took a handful of ash from the fireplace, sprinkled it over the boiling grains, and mixed it thoroughly with both hands. The cockroach realised it was a ruse. Anyu Matli Mu put the boiled mongbree in an earthen pot and covered it. After two days, the lovely smell of fermented brew rose from the pot.

The cockroach thought about the Lepchas and his promise to bring back the buth. He was embarrassed that so many days had passed and he had been unable to get it from Anyu Matli Mu. At last he hit upon a clever idea. Looking at Anyu Matli Mu, he said, 'I can see a lot of lice in your hair. Can I take them out for you?'

The old woman, who seldom had a bath, agreed. The lice were uncomfortable and made her scratch her head all the time. It was winter. She looked for a warm, sunny place to sit and the cockroach began to unbraid her hair. Soon, the warmth of the winter sun and the cockroach's gentle cleaning of her scalp made her drowsy. Anyu Matli Mu fell into a blissful slumber. Seizing his chance, the cockroach carefully removed the small container from around her neck and fled.

When Anyu Matli Mu woke up, she found she had been deceived. Cursing, she shouted, 'You have tricked me. I thought you were my grandson but you turned out to be a thief. From now on, anyone who drinks chee will crave more and more of it, and this will cause quarrels, fights and unpleasantness. It will be good medicine if you know how to drink it but will be poison if you don't.'

By this time, the cockroach was already resting on the serene slopes of Mayel Lyang. As he rested peacefully amid the meadows, a black cobra sneaked up and stole a bit of the buth, which the cockroach was carrying on its back. As soon as he tasted it, the snake went mad and turned poisonous. Next, a honey bee tasted a tiny bit of the buth and he too developed a sharp, nettle-like sting. Some of the larger birds too tasted the buth and turned carnivorous. The small birds who didn't taste it remained vegetarian. The fig tree also touched the buth. As a result, its fruit turned sour. But when the banana plant touched the buth, its fruit tasted sweet. The poison had been removed by the cobra, the honey bee and the large birds. What was left in the buth now was fit for the humans to use. This is the reason why adding buth when making chee turns the brew sweet.

When the tangder finally delivered the buth to Kumsheything, he was very happy. 'You turned out to be the most intelligent among all of us. You shall be rewarded. But first, teach us how Anyu Matli Mu prepares chee.'

When the chee was finally made, Kumsheything took butter from his mother so that he could perform Sakyu Rum Faat for his brother's marriage.

Before Tarbong's family members went to meet Narip

Nom's family, they sent a middleman to inform them of their interest and impending arrival, a tradition continued by the Lepchas. A large group, Tarbong's family, friends and neighbours, carrying a load of gifts, set off towards Sakyong in the mountains. Reaching Narip Nom's home, all the presents were laid down before her. Her mother and uncle finally agreed to give her in marriage to Tarbong. An auspicious date was fixed. All the Gods and men gathered for the marriage. On the wedding day, Narip Nom and Tarbong wore new clothes, a pig was slaughtered, and chee served. All the Lepchas drank the chee, which enabled them to sing, dance and make merry.

ॐ

The customs of Tarbong and Narip Nom's wedding are still followed by the Lepchas. All the Gods are invoked and gifts are prepared for the bride's family. The bongthing narrates the story of how Kumsheything got his brother married, and smearing pago reeps on the foreheads of the newlyweds, blesses them: 'May your nuptial life be fresh, pure and eternal like the pago reep.'

References

1. A prayer of thanksgiving to the Gods of grain.
2. Chee is a fermented, cereal-based mild alcoholic beverage. Here reference is to fermented millet brew.
3. Millet seeds.
4. Also a term of respect and endearment for a senior female.
5. A bumblebee.
6. The Indian trumpet flower, which blooms only at night (also called the broken bones tree).
7. Creeper with a sweet fragrance.
8. A cockroach.

How the Lepchas Got Grain

It is said that in the beginning, when the world was very young, seven divine couples, known to be the ancestors of the Lepchas, lived in seven beautiful houses in Mayel, a mythical village located somewhere near Pun Yeung Chyu, the mountain in front of Kongchen Kongchlo when viewed from Dzongu in north Sikkim. These seven eternal couples are neither considered Gods since they dwell on earth nor humans as they are immortal like the Gods.

Theirs was a paradise of warmth and love, a fairyland of never-ending joy, where crops grew hundred times bigger than elsewhere and where the chirping of birds and the fragrance of flowers filled the air. Itbu-moo had given mongbree, *dumbra*,[1] *ongrey zo*, *kunchung*[2] and many other seeds to these couples. The seeds were to be shared with the Lepchas when the world came to an end, to help rebuild earth.

No human can enter Mayel. Kongchen Kongchlo, standing just behind Pun Yeung Chyu, with its shape like the 'pricked-up ears of an alert animal', guards against the faintest suspicious sound of unwelcome intruders trying to get to the secret village. The Lepchas believe that three spirits—Mayel Yook Rum, also called Pong Rum, the God of hunters, and his younger brothers Mitik and Tomtik—residing on the gates to this secret village guard Mayel.

A long time ago, people from Mayel used to come and mix with the Lepchas living in the foothills of Kongchen Kongchlo. These mystical beings ate and talked like ordinary people. But they stopped visiting when they felt the humans were no longer pious. However, to make up for their absence, they used to send messengers in the form of birds. The kaku announced to the people it was time to sow dryland paddy and other birds announced it was time to harvest the crop. The seven couples also sent migratory birds after winter, a sign that it was time to sow seeds of cucumber, pumpkin and other vegetables.

When the divine people stopped coming to the villages, the Lepchas felt terribly sad. They waited in vain to meet them again. Until one day, a Lepcha shaman suddenly found himself in the secret village of Mayel.

In a small hamlet called Trak Thug Rong, near the present-day Drubdi monastery in west Sikkim, there lived a shaman known as Thekung Mensalung. He spent most of his time toiling in his fields or helping the villagers. Everybody respected him.

Like other men of his hamlet, Thekung Mensalung was very fond of hunting but took to this pastime alone. One autumn afternoon, hunting in a remote forest far away from his village, he came upon a stream. The clear waters of the stream looked inviting and the shaman stopped to quench his thirst. As he bent to take some water in his hands, he saw a tree branch floating in the water. The branch of golden bark had several needle-shaped greenish leaves. Certain that there was no such tree in this stretch of the valley, Thekung Mensalung wondered if the river had brought it down from Mayel.

The shaman felt an eerie sensation after drinking the water and soon found himself trekking up the mountain, following the path of the stream, with his bag of arrows and bow slung over his shoulder. The sun shone brightly and the birds chirped. So excited was he that he forgot all about hunting and kept walking, following the stream. He did not grow tired, thirsty or hungry. He crossed several mountains and valleys covered with thick forests. Sometimes he would see footprints of wild boar and wild cats but saw no sign of the animals. Many days later, he came upon a range of snow-covered mountains. He bowed low before the peaks and offered prayers in honour of the mountain deities.

The shaman continued walking. It was not easy, as the path was covered with dry leaves and branches that were made slippery by the mountain mist. The path got steeper. Sometimes it would disappear and he had to trample on the undergrowth like a blind man, guided by the sound of a waterfall and the intermittent twitter of birds. He reached a great big forest. The trees were very tall and it was dark there; the light was fading. He decided to spend the night under the canopy of trees.

Next morning, he started off again. He had hardly been walking an hour when he stumbled upon another uneven path. This path led him to an open meadow with a lake in the centre. While making a round of the lake, Thekung

Mensalung saw a lot of white feathers and wondered which birds these feathers belonged to. Suddenly, he remembered seeing similar feathers on the birds which came from Mayel bearing messages from the divine people.

Now the shaman was sure he was on the road to Mayel. Following the trail of feathers, he crossed a ridge that led to a green road. After three hours of walking, he reached a green valley carpeted with bright colourful flowers and surrounded by tall mountains with snowy peaks. The shaman showed no signs of exhaustion. He was completely submerged in the beauty of nature. He continued on his journey. He saw tall trees with needle-shaped leaves and golden branches on both sides of the road. Beyond the trees were large fields of grain and vegetables, something peculiar at this high an altitude.

Just as he was wondering where he would spend the night, Thekung Mensalung spotted seven beautiful houses, surrounded by green fields, pretty flowers and trees bearing delicious fruit. Had he finally reached Mayel, the place of his great-great ancestors, thought the shaman.

The sun was already setting when he reached the first house in the valley. The house was quite old. It was round, two-storeyed, with a thatched roof. He could also see fresh signs of the earth dug up by some animals and a lot of feathers, similar to the ones he had seen around the lake, scattered around the house.

He knocked on the door and an old, old woman opened it. Inside, there was a man, just as old, more bent. They invited him inside. The old couple wore dresses woven out of nettle leaves and donned hats made of bamboo and cane. On seeing a stranger, the couple asked, 'O young man, how did you manage to find our house?' The hunter told them how he had followed the stream. 'You have done well, son,' said the old man. 'You can stay here for the night.' The old woman began to prepare some food and chee.

The old man sat on a raised seat and looked outside through a small opening. He began to utter a stream of words the shaman could not understand at all. Is the old man chanting prayers, Thekung Mensalung wondered. Outside, stars filled the sky and the wind whispered through the pine trees. But the shaman did not see the stars nor could he hear the wind.

After a hearty meal, the old woman led him to a clean room with a straw bed which had a new woollen rug. Cool breeze wafted in from a small opening as he lay in the cosy bed. Thekung Mensalung's mind was filled with questions. Did the couple have children or did they live alone? Were they one of the seven divine couples? Soon, he was fast asleep.

When Thekung Mensalung woke the next morning, he could see the sun just behind the mountains, turning the snowy peaks pink and then golden. As he sat watching the sun rise, he heard sounds of children playing and thought they must be the neighbour's.

Presently he asked the children: 'Hello children, do you have any idea where the old couple has gone?'

'Do not panic, O noble sorcerer,' replied the children. 'We are the same old couple. Every morning we become children. By noon, we become adults and as the sun sets, we are old. Next morning, we are children again. This is how our world works.'

The shaman was astonished. He stood still like a rock. At noon, the kids turned into a beautiful, young couple. Thekung Mensalung saw all this as if in a trance, for he was aware of stories of the immortal families who lived in the paradise called Mayel. The young and beautiful couple took Thekung Mensalung around the village to introduce him to the six other couples.

Thekung Mensalung spent seven days in this mythical

land, mesmerised by the beauty of the place. At the end of the seventh day, the first divine couple told him he had to return to his own world as no ordinary human was allowed to live in Mayel for more than seven days.

On the day of his departure, all the families gave him different types of grains, seeds of fruits and vegetables to take back home. 'Sow these seeds in your village, share them with your neighbours and your people will never die of hunger. You will have plenty to eat throughout the year. But remember, sow these seeds at the right time. Never ignore the birds we send to your villages to announce the time for planting the grains. Follow them like you have been doing all these years. And do not tell your people about your visit here. Keep it a secret,' instructed the seven divine couples.

Taking him a little away from the village, they led him to a staircase. 'Go down this staircase and you will find your way back home,' they said, and vanished.

The hunter climbed down the stairs. As he reached the bottom, he developed an intense yearning to see the village he had just visited for one last time. He looked back. But the secret village and the divine couples were no longer there. He did not know where he was, but he soon found himself in the middle of a jungle close to where he had started his journey to Mayel.

His family and friends were happy to see him when he returned. They had all been worried. He distributed the seeds the divine couples had given him among the villagers, and told them to follow the message of the birds.

And this is how the Lepchas came to have grains. To this day, whenever they see flocks of white birds, they know it is time to sow their crops. When they have finished sowing, they pray to their ancestors in Mayel to send them a good harvest.

In reverence to these seven immortal couples, the Lepchas

observe Sakyu Rum Faat, a thanksgiving prayer to the Gods of grain, twice a year. The first prayer takes place just before they embark upon the sowing of the seeds. The second is after they have harvested their crop. The first produce is offered to Sakyu Rum, the God of food.

After his return from Mayel, Thekung Mensalung is said to have lived for over three hundred years and excelled in all his works, including shamanism and literature. The Lepchas visit his grave and pay homage to him with reverence.

References

1. Dryland paddy.
2. Maize.

The Stairway to Heaven

A very long time ago, the Lepchas and a few other tribes like the Bhutias and the Limboos lived together as brothers under the benign presence of Mount Khangchendzonga, in the land where the sun shone all year round. Food was plentiful amidst the valleys and in the streams that flowed from the hills. Everyone led a contented, prosperous life.

One autumn morning, when the sky was blue and the sun was more brilliant than usual, a group of men had a sudden yearning to meet their Gods. So they put together a plan to go up to heaven, where they believed their Gods resided.

'Let us make a ladder to heaven and meet our Gods,' said one of them and the idea pleased everyone.

Another said, 'Let's make big earthen pots and put them one on top of the other to make a column. When the pillar of pots is high enough, we will climb it to reach the heavens and meet our Gods.'

'That will be excellent!' the others said. 'How clever!'

And so they started looking for a suitable site. After days of travelling around the country, the men found a flat piece of land situated to the south of the river Romam in Daramdin in west Sikkim. They named this place Thallom Purtam or a flat land leading upwards.

Soon, all the potters in the land got busy. Some started shaping the clay into pots, others busied themselves collecting wood for lighting the fire in which to bake them, and the rest began the actual work of construction by piling the pots upside down, one over the other. The ladder to heaven went up, and up, and up. Oh, how proud the men were!

The stairway to heaven first rose above the roofs of the houses. Then it went above the treetops. It started to touch the clouds. When it almost touched the sky, the people climbing it could hardly hear each other speak. Some of the Lepcha men in the group, adept in making bamboo crafts and instruments, devised a *passongthop*.[1] When the string holding the instrument was pulled, it would make a certain noise, conveying a message over a considerable distance. They also invented the *blingthop*,[2] which was used to summon potters to work and to tell them when the day's work was over.

When they were almost done, there was a serious breakdown of communication between the artisans working at the top and the ones at the bottom of the earthen-pot tower. The man right on top wanted to know how much further heaven was. So he asked for a hook. He looked down and shouted, '*Kok vim yang ta* (Send up a hooked stick).' The message got passed along down the column. One worker, who could not hear properly, asked, 'What?' '*Kok vim yang ta*,' repeated the man above him, but the other worker heard, '*Cheyk ta* (Smash it down).'

Although the artisans at the top kept yelling, '*Kok vim yang ta*,' by the time the message got through to the bottom, it had become '*Chyek ta*.'

The workers below got very busy. They took their axes and began to hit the pots, smashing them to pieces. 'What's happening?' called the men at the top. Then, there was a noise like thunder. The pots fell down upon each other and upon the men. The stairway to heaven crumbled to the ground, piece by piece, and so did the men. The men's aspiration to meet their Gods remained a dream.

This is how the plains of Thallom Purtam came to be known as Ka Daa Raom Dyen (now called Daramdin), which means 'We ourselves smashed it down'.

References

1. A bamboo instrument split on both sides, held together with bamboo ropes.
2. A smaller version of the passongthop.

The Race between Teesta and Rangeet

Teesta and Rangeet are two major rivers in Sikkim, both emanating from glaciers in the Sikkim Himalayas. Teesta resembles a young woman from the highlands as her sparkling water follows a straight path, traversing through lovely valleys and deep forests. The Rangeet meanders. Why do the two rivers take different paths from the Himalayas and why do they look different before they finally meet in the plains of Bengal and flow together for eternity?

Many, many years ago, before the land of Sikkim was filled with people and when there were no monasteries, the river spirits Rangeet and Rongnyu, revered as Itbu-moo's creations, were much acclaimed throughout the length and breadth of Mayel Lyang, not only for their matchless grace and beauty but for their apparent love for one another. They were never seen apart and went everywhere in each other's company.

The two river spirits used to meet secretly in a place high in the cloud-cloaked, snow-shrouded lap of the Himalayas. But when their love was known to all, they offered salutations to Kongchen Kongchlo and decided to go away, very far, unseen by their friends. However, as if to conceal their sacred love, the river spirits decided to take different routes, promising to meet at Pozok.[1] They issued a playful challenge to each other—their journey would be a race down to the distant plains.

Since the two spirits were venturing beyond the sacred environs of their home for the first time, they did not know the paths they were to travel. The lovers agreed to take a guide each on their long journey.

Being male, Rangeet was competitive, wanting to win against everybody, including his own lover. Rangeet chose tutfo, a mountain bird, to guide him to the plains. He knew the bird was the swiftest and would help him win the race. Rongnyu, was more subdued, milder and pleasant. She decided to follow parilbu, a snake. Wishing each other well, as good friends do even when they are competing against each other, the river spirits set off.

The bird, while swift, would get distracted by the abundant fruit on the trees, the colourful flowers, or strange-looking insects. All these caught its fancy and it would wander off to play with other birds or to eat some fruit. Sometimes, it would rest awhile to enjoy the myriad colours of the forest. Rangeet followed the meandering, procrastinating tutfo, longing to meet Rongnyu, yet bound to his guide. Intent on winning, he constantly reminded the tutfo of the race but the bird would never listen to him.

True to its nature, the snake darted straight as an arrow

down to the plains, without looking left or right, intent on reaching the destination. Following the snake, Rongnyu was soon in sight of the plains. She knew she had won the race, but her happiness gave way to concern as she waited and waited for her lover.

When Rangeet eventually rolled out from a steep mountain crag, he sighted Rongnyu far below him. He raged swiftly, pulling huge chunks of mud to reach the destination ahead of his lover. But Rongnyu was already there. His first words on seeing her were, '*Thi-see-tha* (When did you arrive)?' When he realised he had come in second, his pride was hurt. It was intolerable! A trick of fate! Enraged because he had lost the race to a female, Rangeet decided to flow back to the Himalayas. He cried and groaned, threw himself on the ground and struck himself with such force that he began to flow back to the Himalayas causing destruction everywhere.

On seeing her lover's anger, Rongnyu was grief-stricken. She decided to follow him, begging him not to go back. As a result, the waters of the rivers rose higher and higher.

In the valley, the people had forgotten what they owed Itbu-moo and had stopped offering sacrifices and prayers to her. Legend has it that it was Mother Creator who triggered this deluge to remind the people of the need to worship her. The rising waters of the two rivers flooded the land, causing forests, hills and even mountains to disappear under it. Men, women and children, animals, birds and insects climbed trees and went higher up the mountains, crying out for help.

And still the waters rose.

Only Tundong Lho, a mountain in Damthang in south Sikkim, did not get flooded. The mountain rose higher and higher to save the Lepchas, who had climbed it to save themselves from the great deluge. Seeing the devastation and realising it was a sign of Itbu-moo's wrath, the people who had taken refuge on Tundong Lho came together and tried to appease her by offering special sacrifices, burning incense and reciting prayers. 'Save us, O Mother Creator. We know you are unhappy with us. This flood is a sign of your unhappiness. Please forgive us.' But their prayers were in vain.

At last, kahomfo, the partridge, reached the peak of Tundong Lho and made an offering of mongbree, which it had brought wrapped in a huge leaf. Facing Kongchen Kongchlo, it tossed the grains upwards in the sky, praying and pleading for mercy. The bird's sincere appeal on behalf of the creatures of earth was heard. Itbu-moo relented. The partridge carries white dots on its plumage from the scattered mongbree that fell upon him during his oblation.

Itbu-moo's sudden change of mood caused a huge tremor, forcing the floods to recede. All the creatures were able to descend from Tundong Lho and resume their former lives, always remembering to worship the mountain, Tundong Lho, which had saved so many lives.

Rongnyu, who would not accept her lover leaving her, decided to woo her beloved Rangeet back. 'Do not be vexed, my darling,' she pleaded. 'It is not your fault. You arrived late because of your guide.' In spite of his rage, Rangeet heard his lover's sweet soothing voice and stopped. Rongnyu caught up with him and the two rivers fell into a long embrace, united at last, flowing down to the plains of Bengal, never to be parted again. Later, Rongnyu came to be known as Thi-see-tha or Teesta.

When the Lepchas heard the story of the two river spirits, they flocked to the confluence of the two rivers as pilgrims to make offerings to the river Gods. The Lepcha bride and bridegroom are always taken to the rivers Teesta and Rangeet and people wish the newlywed couple a happy and prosperous life like the two river spirits.

References

1. Literally, a deep forest. Present-day Pesok in north Bengal.

The Sun and the Moon

$\mathcal{M}$uch before Itbu-moo shaped the first man from a ball of fresh snow, she created mountains and lakes, plants and animals, rivers and forests. And then Mother Creator said, 'Let there be light in the world.' And there were two suns.

'The two of you should come out in turns,' instructed Itbu-moo. 'The older of you should come out in the mornings and the younger at night.' Because of the kind of work entrusted to them, she decorated the sky with countless stars, clouds and other heavenly bodies as gifts for the two brothers. Happy with such beautiful creations in their midst, the two brothers then built a palace where they lived together, each loving and respecting the other. The two never had misunderstandings and shared their work willingly. Unfortunately, this quiet, idyllic routine was not destined to last forever.

With the constant presence of two suns, the people of the world were put to great inconvenience. They did not know when to work, take rest or go to sleep. Forests shrivelled, lakes dried up and rivers shrunk due to the heat generated by two suns.

So one day, the humans, animals and other beings of the earth came together to find a solution to their common problem. 'If we do not do something, we may soon die because of the suns' constant heat upon us,' said a group of men. Some nodded in support while there were others who suggested staying under the shade of trees. 'What if the trees themselves die from the heat?' There seemed to be no end to their worries.

After a prolonged discussion, they came to the unanimous decision that one of the suns had to be killed. 'If one sun is not killed, the world will be destroyed. We have got to live.' Volunteers were called for to kill one sun.

Three days passed. A week went by. But no one came forward. Eventually lukpok tuluk, a mountain frog, volunteered. He bragged that he would return only after killing the sun. But when he reached the sun, the proud frog could do nothing, and even lost his thumbs in his attempt to kill the sun. Ashamed that he was unsuccessful, he decided to live in the high altitudes, adapting himself to life there, so that others could not see him.

Next to volunteer was dar tuluk, another mountain frog. The monsoon had just receded and the *kutneum*[1] had grown tall. Carving a bow from this plant, the frog aimed an arrow at the sun and killed the older of the two. The sun died at once. Oh! How happy the beings on earth were. What they didn't realise then was that their happiness was short-lived.

Being the older of the two, the heat of the dead sun was stronger.

The younger sun, on seeing his dead brother, went into mourning. '*Kasu anum labo* (Give back my brother),' he cried out in great agony. But the humans on earth were too busy rejoicing to hear his cries. In great sorrow, the younger brother pulled a black cloak over himself and refused to come out. Now the whole world was thrown into perpetual darkness. There was much fear and shedding of tears among the humans.

Overtaken with remorse, everyone called out to the younger sun and prayed to him to come out and lighten up the days. But the younger sun could not forgive the creatures of the earth so easily. Pained by the loss of his elder brother, his only reply was, '*Kasu anum labo.*'

As a result of the perpetual night, the wooden mortars kept in the courtyards turned into tigers while the wooden pestles looked like serpents and snakes. They started killing people. There was complete darkness all around. No work could be done. The fireflies tried to bring light, but it was inadequate for all the beings on earth. The *numbum* tree also tried to use its whitish leaves to light up the world, but was unsuccessful.

Men, the more intelligent among all the creatures, convened a meeting to think of ways and means of getting out of this calamity which they had created. 'We must persuade the younger sun to come back. For us to survive in this world, everyone should go personally and appeal to him to come out,' suggested the men. One after another, all men and other living creatures tried their best to coax the younger sun. They all failed. The only creature now left to take its turn was a tiny bat. Nobody believed that this puny creature would succeed. They gave up all hope of staying alive on earth.

Before going to meet the sun, the bat said, 'All my fellow

beings underneath the heavens, I am prepared to go to the sun and expose myself to all sorts of dangers for your sake. I am also prepared to lose myself because of your faults and failings. But who am I to stand before such a royal being as the sun? I am only a desperate, tiny creature.'

'Come what may, you will have to persuade the sun to come back. You are the only one left now,' said all the other creatures.

In despair, the bat went and hung itself on the door of the sun's house. It kept drinking its own urine, making a constant, squeaky *chuk chuk chuk* noise. The sun had heard several entreaties before but never one like this. What a peculiar sound it was! Out of curiosity, the sun lifted the black blanket to take a peek at the bat. And he saw the suffering on earth.

On seeing the sun, the bat started pleading, entreating him to shine again. 'O King, I am the last being on earth to plead before you. If you don't listen to me, the earth will shrivel up. It will die. I seek pardon for all the injustices and transgressions of man and other beings on earth. Please come out and make us happy,' pleaded the bat in a small voice.

Barely had he said these words, the poor bat, being too close to the sun, got charred by the sun's heat and fell from its perch onto the hard ground below—the reason why a bat's legs and hands look all broken. The Lepchas believe this is also the reason why bats come out only at night.

When the humans and other creatures saw the younger sun showing a bit of his face, all of them decided to assemble before him and plead. 'O saviour of the world, the whole world was thrown into darkness when you went into mourning. All creatures live in great anxiety and fear without your presence. Unless you come back, there will be no peace on earth. Come out for us, O saviour, and brighten up our lives.'

Touched by the plea made in harmony, the sun decided to come out, but on certain conditions. 'Listen, O beings of the earth, I will come out only if you promise me that you will do something so that my dead brother will always be remembered,' said the younger sun.

The humans and other beings were so demoralised and desperate that they agreed to this condition. The younger sun came out and brightened up the earth once again. All the creatures were happy and there were celebrations all around.

And to fulfil the younger sun's condition, the older sun became the moon.

References

1. A red-stemmed vegetable plant.

How the Cat Began to Live with Man

$\mathcal{I}$t all began a long time ago when an old monk, after months of isolation in the forest, returned home only to find that all his clothes and foodstuffs had been gnawed by the rats. The rats had nibbled on everything their tiny, sharp teeth could get hold of in the monk's storeroom. With nothing left to eat, the old monk shouted: 'You wretched creatures of the earth! How dare you eat away all my food and nibble on my clothes! Why have you upset me like this? I've got nothing to eat now and I am very hungry.' But to the monk's astonishment, the rats denied eating the things in his house.

To make sure the rats were the real

culprits, the monk set a trap for the animals that evening. When the monk went to bed, a bevy of rats entered the monk's larder and ate some of the food. Next morning, the monk was not surprised to see a rat in the trap. Angry, the old monk took out the rat and cut off his whiskers and tail as punishment before flinging it into the gutter. 'Now try and eat my food as much as you like!' he said in anger.

'This is downright cruelty, old monk,' proclaimed the injured rat. 'The king may have harsh rules against wrongdoers but no one dare cut off anyone's whiskers like you have done to me. And the tails of animals should never be cut off. Even though you are a pious man, you have done both. I cannot forget this. I will call all my family members and friends and will declare war on you. From now on, we will harm you as much as we want. No one can save you from us. Just wait and watch.'

'O go away!' replied the monk testily. 'If you harm me, I will pray to the Gods in heaven and ask them for protection.' While the injured rat ran to summon his friends and family members, the monk went into seclusion to pray to the Gods in heaven to protect him from the clutches of the rats.

The Gods listened to his prayers and sent down the cat, wrapped in dough, with special instructions to protect the old monk from those troublesome rats. By this time, the injured rat had also brought together all his friends and family. When the monk opened his eyes on completing his meditation, all he could see was rats and more rats. Rats here, rats there, everywhere!

A family of rats living near the old monk's house did not approve of what the other rats had been doing. Going up to the army of rats assembled around the monk's house, the head of the family said, 'Listen, my brothers, do not get upset with me, but we should never nibble on the monk's robe nor eat his food. If we do so, we are bound to suffer and trouble will come our way.' But the rat whose tail and whiskers had been cut off, was in no mood to listen to this advice. 'Stop your nonsense!' he retorted. 'I am the boss here. Your talk is of no use.'

All the gathered rats then entered the monk's house and began to stay there permanently. Poor old monk! He had a tough time with the rats eating away at all the food. But he just sat still, albeit apprehensively, waiting for the cat to make its move.

Just like the gentle monk, the cat sat quietly in the corner of the room for many days. Then, at certain times, he would scamper off to inspect the larder. It was a big one. He was thrilled. This would be a good hunting ground for him! When he heard the rats squeak, he would hide behind a corner and wait to pounce. When a rat came into the larder, the cat didn't waste any time. He sprung on the rat and grasped it in his mouth and bit it with his sharp teeth. In this way, hundreds of rats were killed.

The cat grew tired of waiting for the rats for hours on end and devised a plan. With hundreds of them already killed, the rats were ready to listen to the cat in order to save their lives. Gradually, the cat became the boss and directed the rats to bring water and food for him. As the rats took their turn to take food and water to the cat, they were killed by the cat. None of the rats would return. The remaining rats grew suspicious of the cat. Where had their friends who had gone to deliver the food and water to the cat disappeared? It looked fatter and healthier as the days passed. Soon, all the rats were killed except one who was expecting a baby. She ran away.

One morning, the cat found the monk praying to the Gods, thanking them for sending this saviour, the cat. The monk took the cat on his lap and let him sleep. But the cat knew his job would never be over. He could not sleep peacefully. He would always have to look out for the one rat that had escaped. She would have given birth to other rats.

The Lepchas believe that if the cat had killed and eaten that one last rat too, then the earth would have been free of rats and the cat would have gone back to heaven. But because one rat had survived, the cat had to stay back, to keep an eye on the monk's larder and his clothes. That is why cats are never killed by man. Lepchas firmly believe that killing a cat is a big sin as the animal is supposed to have descended from heaven. It is also said that the purring of the cat is the animal's prayer to the Gods.

The Bird
with the
Golden Beak

$\mathcal{A}$ very long time ago, Itbu Debu Rum, head of the male Gods in Rum Lyang, called all the lesser Gods in front of him to ask a question which had been plaguing him for quite some time. 'Pay attention, all you Rums.[1] Have you been hearing someone from earth saying prayers in a deeply sweet tone?' Itbu Debu Rum asked.

'Yes, yes,' replied the Gods. 'We have also been bothered by the same call for a long time. These sweet supplications are usually heard during dawn and dusk.'

Itbu Debu Rum summoned the Rumveeks[2] for a mission. 'Listen Rumveeks,' he ordered, 'there is someone in the mortal world praying fervently to us every day in the morning and evening. Go down, take your time, search everywhere for that sweet singing being. Test the creature, hear its melodious supplication and then bring it to me. Consider this a priority.'

Immediately the Rum-veeks descended to earth and busied themselves, travelling through the human world, searching for the sweet-singing devotee. They traversed wooded paths, dales and valleys, crossed several streams and lakes but did not find the creature.

They started enquiring among the humans, birds, beasts and other beings whom they met on their travels. Finally, a toad, who had heard that such a search for a singing devotee was on, said: 'Messengers of the Gods, listen to me. I am the one who has been praying to Itbu Debu Rum in the mornings and evenings, and even at night.'

Happy that they had found the singing devotee, the Rum-veeks took the toad to Rum Lyang. But before presenting him to the head of the Gods, he was kept in a corner for some time. The Rum-veeks wanted to hear the sounds before taking the toad to Itbu Debu Rum.

Itbu Debu Rum was aware that a creature had been brought by the Rum-veeks and was in their midst, and yet he continued to hear the same sweet voice of supplication coming from the human world. Turning to the other Gods, he said, 'I am sure the Rum-veeks have brought someone here but I can still hear the same melodious voice from below.'

'Yes, so can we,' replied the other Gods.

When the toad started croaking, the Rum-veeks quickly brought the animal before the Gods. On hearing the toad's rough, jarring, discordant note, Itbu Debu Rum caught hold of the toad and flung it back to earth in anger. The poor toad landed on a stinging nettle bush on its back, with its four legs up in the air, which is why the Lepchas believe the back of the toad appears rough, swollen and blistered.

Itbu Debu Rum was upset. Once again he ordered the Rum-veeks to go down to earth. 'This is no joke,' he shouted at the Rum-veeks. 'Take your time but find me the correct creature this time, or else I will throw all of you out of heaven. Now leave.' The smaller Gods in heaven grew concerned. To ensure the Rum-veeks were successful this time, they descended to earth along with some fairies to help find the melodious devotee.

Down in the realm of men and animals, the heavenly beings called upon all the birds, beasts and other creatures to sing their prayers in front of them, one by one. On judgement day, the chamongfo[3] turned out to be the best singer. 'Surely this must be the voice that Itbu Debu Rum has been hearing for so many days,' the Gods thought. The heavenly beings then took the bird to Rum Lyang.

The bird was presented before Itbu Debu Rum. Itbu Debu Rum and all the other Gods were deeply touched and pleased by the chamongfo's sweet singing tone. All the Gods shed tears of joy. And as a reward, Itbu Debu Rum turned the bird to gold, shiny and bright. The chamongfo then returned to earth.

For a time, the chamongfo lived the life of a king inside a golden palace. Here he felt safe from the threat of bigger birds and humans. But soon he grew bold. Basking in its newfound blessing, the bird wanted to show off his beauty. He ventured out to springs or streams to take a bath and would sit on rocks, showing off his golden wings to everyone who passed by.

The other birds who saw him were jealous of his golden body and shiny beak. They thought the chamongfo was becoming too arrogant. They wanted to teach him a lesson. One day, when the chamongfo came out to bathe in a stream, all the other birds surrounded him. The chamongfo managed to fly away but the other birds gave chase over hills and dales, rivers and forests. The chamongfo began to feel tired. He came upon a marshy ground and to save himself from his enemies, landed in the swamp, wading in among the reeds. The golden bird tried to run fast in the swamp but was unable to walk in the muddy waters and resigned himself to his fate. While standing there panting for breath, he wanted to save his beak and neck so that he could continue singing his prayers. He submerged his beak deep down into the swampy mud and closing his eyes, started praying to the Gods. The other birds started pecking at him and all the gold that covered his body came off.

After some time, thinking that the proud bird was now dead, the other birds left him and flew away. After many hours, when the chamongfo regained consciousness, he waded out of the swamp, completely exhausted. Seeing how dirty he was, he flew to a nearby spring and started washing off the mud that covered his entire body. To his great sorrow, he found that in place of the gold, his body had turned a deep, dark blue, bruised from the pecking by the other birds. Only his beak, which he had submerged in the mud for protection, still retained the gold given by the Gods. This made him somewhat happy. 'I will sing again,' he resolved, 'to thank the Gods for protecting me.'

That is why, today, the chamongfo has a peacock-blue body. It is always seen flying in the mornings and evenings near brooks and streams. Perhaps it hopes that one day, while washing itself, the gold will be restored over the rest of its body.

And the bird still sings the same melodious tune that so pleases the Rums.

References

1. Lepcha term for the gods.
2. The attendants of the gods.
3. A large, blue-black Himalayan whistling thrush with a bright, deep blue forehead, wings and tail.

The Orphan Boy and the River Nymph

*I*n the days of old, when animals talked like humans, and Gods and fairies still frequented the human world, there lived an orphan boy. His home was a small hut located on the banks of the river Teesta. He had barely enough to live by and remained unemployed most of the time. He used to fish for his food, since the river would remain full of fish all year round.

He rose before dawn and worked very hard through the day catching fish. This daily chore not only kept the orphan boy out of mischief but also made his life a very solitary one. Everybody in the village liked him but he was too busy working all day to feed himself and seldom visited them. Exhausted after the day's work, he would hardly have the energy to spend the evening with other boys in the village. He always went to bed early so that he was well-rested to work the next day.

One day, the boy happened to catch a very big fish. He had never caught such a big fish before and was happy that this fish would be enough to feed him for several days. 'Great! I can take a break for a few days!' the boy breathed a sigh of relief. He put away his fishing rod, and as he lay there pondering how to cut his catch, the fish spoke. 'Do not kill me, O young man,' beseeched the fish. 'My parents will grieve badly if you take my soul away. Instead, why don't you come with me? I will take you to my parents in the river. They will be happy to see you.'

Confused, the boy answered, 'But how can I go with you into the deep waters just to see your parents? Also, I cannot swim very well.'

'Do not worry. All you need to do is hold on to my tail and jump into the water with me,' said the fish.

The boy, tired of his life of daily struggle, was ready to try out an adventure. So he dived into the waters, holding on tightly to the tail of the fish. In no time the fish led the boy to her parents. To the boy's amazement, the father fish was seated on a golden throne and the mother fish on a silver throne. As the gold and silver thrones glittered in the water, the orphan boy stood marvelling at the strange vision.

'Dear mother and father, this boy is an orphan. He is a good friend of mine. Today he did not kill me after catching me. Since he was so very kind to me, I have brought him here to see both of you,' explained the fish.

'That was very kind of you young man, to save our daughter today. Thank you very much,' said the parents.

'Both of us are very happy and we would like to recompense you for your kind gesture. What would you like to have? Tell us and we shall give it to you right away.'

The orphan boy had seen a small, white puppy lying in one corner of the glittering palace. When he heard he could get whatever he asked for, he asked for the puppy.

That evening the boy returned to his hut with his puppy. He washed himself, stoked the fire and cooked his meal. Then he tied the puppy in one corner, gave it some food and threw a light cloth over its back before going to bed. The next morning, the boy had to leave in search of the day's food. In his rush, he forgot about the puppy.

In the evening, as the boy approached his hut, he could smell something unusual in the air. When he opened the front door, he saw a fire lit in the hearth. The room was spick and span, as if it had been swept, and when he went to the kitchen, the food had already been cooked. 'This is incredible!' he thought. The delicious aroma from the pan was too tempting to resist, and he ate all the food, for he was very hungry. Never had he gone to sleep with his stomach so full.

It was the same the next evening, and the next. For several days there was food cooked and his hut cleaned when he returned home in the evenings. The boy began to worry. Who comes and takes care of my house, he wondered. Could it be the village girls who tease me when I go to fish early in the morning? I must find out who it is. This cannot carry on for long, he told himself. That night he fell asleep while thinking of a plan.

The next morning, the orphan boy got ready and left his hut as usual. But after walking a short distance, he turned around and backtracked. This time he approached his house from the back. He settled down to wait and watch through a hole in the wall.

The orphan boy waited for a long time. Just when he

thought no one was going to come, to his utter bewilderment he saw a stunningly beautiful woman emerge from the puppy tied in the corner. 'Oh my God! How is this possible?!' he exclaimed.

The boy stared wide-eyed at the unusual beauty. She was golden from head to waist and silver from waist downwards. Her golden hair cascaded down to her heels. Her brilliant eyes shone.

He saw her sweep the floor, light the fire in the hearth, clean the pots and prepare the evening meal, oblivious of his presence. He felt as if he was in dream. Already in love with the girl, he did not want the fairy-like girl to vanish. Suddenly, he ran into the house. Grasping the puppy, he tore the skin to pieces and scattered it everywhere. Gold and silver flowers rained down.

'Who are you?' he asked. 'Where did you come from? And what do you want?'

'I am the daughter of the river Gods, the river nymph who took you to see them,' she said.

From that day, the river nymph started to live with the orphan boy in his cottage as his wife. When this news reached the villagers, they rushed to get a glimpse of the girl. Soon, the couple became everyone's envy. The news about the orphan boy and his beautiful nymph wife even reached the king.

One day the king decided to go and see her for himself. When he reached the orphan's hut, he was astonished by the beauty and grace of the river nymph. He immediately fancied her and wanted to marry her. How can this stupid boy keep such a pretty woman in this hut, thought the king.

The king came up to the hut and announced a competition to be held between the boy and him. 'Let us undertake a rooster fight and whoever wins shall get the nymph.' The contest was fixed for the next morning at sunrise. The poor orphan boy had no choice but to accept the king's challenge for how could he disobey his king?

Having agreed to the fight, the orphan boy sat in one corner of his hut and began to weep bitterly. 'I am a poor man and don't even have a small bird. With what will I fight the king's powerful rooster?' the orphan boy told his wife. His wife came to his rescue. 'Do not worry, beloved. Just go to the river and meet my parents and ask them for a medium-size rooster.'

The orphan boy went to the river and in no time returned with a medium-size rooster.

At sunrise the next day, both the king's powerful rooster and the boy's middle-size rooster were let loose on the playing ground. Not very long into the fight, the king's rooster was killed.

'Since you have won the contest today,' roared the king, 'we will have a bull fight tomorrow.'

The boy returned home crestfallen even though he had won the rooster fight. 'Where can I get a bull to fight?' he told his wife. 'Go to my parents,' she consoled him, 'and ask them for a medium-size bull.' Again he went down to the stream, swam across the currents and came back with a bull.

The next morning the two bulls started fighting and the king's bull was killed very soon. This made the king very angry. 'This is unbelievable! How can this happen? How can this orphan win? I cannot let this happen. We will now fight with armies,' ordered the king.

This time the orphan boy wept louder than ever for he knew there was no way he could challenge the king's army. Am I really going to lose my wife for good, he thought. The king had an entire army and he was alone.

But the beautiful girl would never betray the orphan boy. 'Beloved, you have to go to my parents for the last time and request them for a medium-size box,' she said.

As usual, the boy did not return empty-handed from the abode of the river Gods.

Next morning at sunrise, when he saw the king coming towards him with a big army, he opened the box. Lightning flashed out of it, killing the king and all his men in an instant.

Legend has it that the orphan boy then became the king and lived happily ever after with the river nymph as his wife, ruling the land with compassion.

The Cave of the Occult Fairies

*I*t was the second half of the eighth century. In the ancient country of Tibet, Guru Padmasambhava, the great Indian tantric master known to the Sikkimese people as Guru Rinpoche,[1] or the precious master, was almost through with his spiritual works. One bright sunny day, before his departure from Tibet, the master shot an arrow from Tibet to mark the spot where a new kingdom, akin to paradise, would arise.

To know where the arrow had landed, the tantric master closed his eyes, going into a meditational trance. Within a few seconds he saw a conical hill rising from a deep gorge dividing the river Rangeet from Rathong Chu, which rises from the south face of

Mount Khangchendzonga. The arrow had landed on a rock, which had turned white. The tantric master christened this spot Thakkar Tashiding or the 'white-spotted fortunate mound', which can be found in west Sikkim.

Padmasambhava set forth from Tibet with twenty-five of his closest disciples. A demon couple followed the tantric's entourage to foil his spiritual work. When the tantric master initiated his rituals at Tashiding, the demon couple began their evil work. The male demon transformed himself into a giant snake and reared his head from the ground near the spot where Padmasambhava was performing his rituals.

Intermittently, the male demon would emit a poisonous gas from its mouth in order to defile the spiritual aura. The tantric master would retaliate immediately. A fierce battle between good and evil thus ensued. Eventually the male demon was killed. With his powers, Padmasambhava immediately converted the body of the dead snake into a rock, which can be seen as a cut rock at the back of the sacred stupa known as Choedten Thongwa Rangdrol, which means 'deliverance by mere sight'.

Fearing a similar fate, the demon wife ran southwards following the river Rangeet. The tantric master knew letting the demon wife live would create havoc in the world and so he made up his mind to finish her as well. Tracing the clues along the course of the river, he chased her until he came to a cave located on the right bank of the river. 'I'm sure the demon wife has taken shelter inside this cave,' said Padmasambhava.

Sitting at the mouth of the cave, he began to chant mantras. He also put a triangular magic fence around the area up to the river and gently called for the demon to come out. A little later, the demon came out of the cave and tried to run away but failed to break through the magic fence.

Meanwhile, the tantric master had decided to enter the

cave through a low entrance at the bottom of a hill. He sat down to meditate for a night inside the cave, to enhance his spiritual power to help him subjugate the demon. Throughout the night the demon tried to escape but could not cross the magic fence. She became desperate and her evil mind came up with a plan to kill the tantric master. While Padmasambhava was still inside the cave, the demon began to erect a rock dam across the river hoping to kill him by flooding the cave.

It was afternoon by the time Padmasambhava was through with his meditation. He knew this would be an appropriate time to attack the demon, for demons tend to lose their powers around sunset. The tantric master came out of the cave to kill the demon but to his horror saw her building a stone wall in the river. It was almost half-done.

'What have you been doing all day in the middle of that fearsome river?' the master enquired.

'I am building a bridge so that I can run across,' the demon replied, hiding her true motive.

Suspecting the demon's plot to kill him instead, the tantric master went up to her and befriended her. He knew there was no other way to bring the demon under his power than by pretending to care for her. 'Dear, there's no need for you to build a bridge. The river is so frighteningly big it may engulf you anytime. Come here, stay with me. Be my wife and I will take care of you,' he cajoled. The demon wife, who had been left alone after her husband's death, believed the tantric master.

The sun began to set in the distant horizon. This was a perfect time for Padmasambhava to lure the demon towards him and kill her. Bringing her up from the river, he embraced her. Then he laid her down on a flat rock just in front of the cave. The moment the demon slipped into an intoxicated state of mind, the tantric master stabbed her heart with his *vajrakila*, a mystic dagger. So powerful was the dagger, it even pierced the rock beneath her. This rock with the physical imprint of the demon is still visible and is known as Sinmo Tuldo or 'the stone where the demon was subdued'. Half the dam which the demon tried to build can be seen in the middle of the Rangeet. It seems to float on the river's surface and is known as Sinmo Sampo or the demon bridge.

Shivering with pain, the demon tried to rise. The master took out the magic dagger again and chopped her body into bits to destroy her completely. The task wasn't easy even for the master. While cutting up the demon's body, one of the pieces from her thigh slipped into the river. The piece of flesh immediately turned into a fish and swam downstream. Padmasambhava was certain the demon had taken her soul into her thigh which is why she was able to transform herself into a fish. He instantly transformed himself into an otter, jumped into the river and began to chase the fish.

The chase continued for quite some time. Just when the otter was about to catch the fish in its mouth, the fish jumped out of the water, landed on the sand, shrugged its slippery body thrice, turned into a wild boar and fled towards the northern mountains. Padmasambhava transformed himself back into his human form and following the clues, reached the top of Tsun Byak, a low hill situated between Tashiding and Pemayangtse. Through his spiritual powers he produced a bow and arrow to kill the boar. The chase continued.

Climbing the steep, craggy banks of Rathong Chu, where ordinary men would fear to tread, Padmasambhava finally found the wild boar in a place called Tseram. Sensing the tantric master's presence, the demon hid herself in a chasm. This the tantric master spotted and without delay released an arrow, killing the boar instantly. Afterwards, he set fire in the chasm and destroyed the body.

On his way back to Tashiding hill, he planted the bow on

top of Tsun Byak, which exists today in the form of a bamboo grove. The people of the surrounding villages believe that this bamboo is the best for making a bow because it is blessed by Padmasambhava.

As evidence of the guru's meditation inside the cave on the banks of the river Rangeet, an imprint of the mystic dagger on the left wall of the cave was discovered. Similarly, on the right wall were figures of five *khandroma* or *dakinis*, perhaps other demons which had followed Padmasambhava. The tantric master is believed to have subjugated these demons and made them guardian angels of the cave. The cave later came to be known as Khandro Sangphug, or the cave of the occult fairies. It lies to the east of Tashiding and is also called Lho Khandro Sangphug or the eastern cave.

As evidence of the demon wife being chopped by the tantric master with his mystic dagger, the heart and lungs of the demon were discovered hung on the roof of the cave amid mystic patterns. Just below these figures is a strange-looking rock, which is believed to be the vase of longevity surrounded by seven kinds of offerings. Legend has it that other parts of the demon's body chopped by Padmasambhava's magic dagger are buried underneath this vase. A square shaped stone nearby is described as the *mandala*[2] and to the east of this lies the seven *norbu samphel* or mind-glowing gems and a methodological text for the propitiation of fairies. There is a tunnel in the cave, ten to twelve yards long and barely two to three feet in height. This narrow tunnel leads to the sanctum sanctorum of the cave where Padmasambhava is known to have meditated to acquire his powers. A deep imprint of his seat where he sat in meditation and an impression of the master's crown are visible on the roof of the sanctum sanctorum.

Khandro Sangphug is virtually a heavenly abode of the fairies. The remains of the demons and images of fairies are still visible in the cave and its surroundings. Devotees make it a point to visit this cave once a year to pray to Padmasambhava, their precious master, to continue protecting them from demons and evil. They are firm in their belief that their noble wishes and dreams will be fulfilled.

References

1. Guru Rinpoche is revered as the patron saint of Sikkim.
2. Literally, centre or circumference or the universe with the palace of the deity at the centre; here, reference is to the visualised ideal universe.

How Jhyo Rathey and Aandhi Phoda Got Separated

Jhyo[1] Rathey or Tinjhurey hill[2] falls within the Fambonglha Wildlife Sanctuary in the East District of Sikkim on the left of the road from Thangkha village to Martam. This hill is composed of three dome-like rocks and is surrounded by other smaller hills and thick forests, making it look like a sovereign amidst courtiers.

Aandhi Phoda is south of Jhyo Rathey, also in the East District, about thirty kilometres away. This much broader hill of loam, deciduous trees and dark boulders stands alone and seems to rise from the river like a giant. The two hills are today separated by a village, river and highway.

The Lepchas believe that the two hills at one time were next to each other. Both hills are believed to be the dwelling places of two powerful mountain spirits—Jhyo Rathey and Aandhi Phoda. Of the two mountain spirits, Jhyo Rathey, the elder one, was responsible for ensuring timely rainfall in the area. Of Aandhi Phoda, nothing much is known, except that he was gentler in his ways, though as powerful as Jhyo Rathey. For many years the two friends lived happily next to each other. Sometimes they used to have heated altercations as all friends do.

Aandhi Phoda fell in love with Jhyo Rathey's daughter, Thasey,[3] and wanted to marry her. Jhyo Rathey, however, refused when Aandhi Phoda asked for Thasey's hand in marriage. Known to be the king of the local spirits, Jhyo Rathey did not like the idea of a subordinate marrying his daughter. Thasey and Aandhi Phoda decided to get married against her father's wishes. This made Jhyo Rathey very angry and he threw a table at Aandhi Phoda, hitting him on his chest.

Aandhi Phoda lived in a place strewn with large boulders. Picking a longish stone, he flung it at Jhyo Rathey in retaliation. Unfortunately, as Jhyo Rathey was taller, the stone dropped halfway.

But it was not easy for Jhyo Rathey to digest his friend's guts. 'How dare you throw a stone at me? Who are you to marry my daughter? You are subordinate to me!' raged Jhyo Rathey. All the junior spirits residing on smaller hills below Jhyo Rathey began to worry. They sensed something catastrophic was going to happen.

Jhyo Rathey wanted to create obstacles in the way, knowing Aandhi Phoda would do anything to meet Thasey. He kicked his right leg, thereby creating a hill and a lake. Even this did not cool his anger. Thunderstorms followed by heavy rains began to rage down like never before. Rivers overflowed their banks and landslides occurred in the villages. The storm wreaked so much devastation that men fled their homes to save their lives.

The lesser Gods went to Aandhi Phoda and asked him to seek Jhyo Rathey's forgiveness. Seeing the devastation caused by the thunderstorms and the people suffering, Aandhi Phoda agreed to appease Jhyo Rathey. He sacrificed animals and birds in honour of Jhyo Rathey, pleading for forgiveness. But Jhyo Rathey could not forgive Aandhi Phoda and cursed him. The only way his anger could be appeased was if Aandhi Phoda moved away, far away from Thasey.[4]

No one looked at Thasey again. And in memory of her beloved, Thasey never married, remaining a virgin. People believe that a convent built at the top of Thasey is proof that she never married and where she spent the rest of her days.

Aandhi Phoda carries the marks of the table injuring him on his chest in the form of a huge landslide scar.

References

1. Honorific Bhutia title meaning respected or reverend; also great-great-ancestor.
2. Three-humped hillock.
3. The name thasey is derived from an ornamental tree, *Erythrina indica* (Indian coral tree), which grows abundantly on this hill.
4. Thasey is located seven kilometres south of Jhyo Rathey, and Aandhi Phoda thirty kilometres south of Jhyo Rathey. From his vantage height, Jhyo Rathey keeps a watchful eye on these two lower mountains.

A Tale of Two Trees

The story of Lali Guras or rhododendron[1] and how he ventured out of the confines of his picturesque environs to seek a suitable bride is not only a favourite among huntsmen, shepherds and cowherds, but is also a story that has moved the hearts of many a lover.

It was springtime. Blossoming flowers decorated the forests. The green stretches of the Himalayas above eight thousand feet had given way to a riot of colours. The flowers on the branches of the rhododendron trees filled the valley with a sweet fragrance.

Lali Guras, a young, male rhododendron, had grown up into a handsome plant. He was completely covered in bright pink flowers. All eyes were on him. Seeing his splendour, friends and neighbours tried to coax Lali Guras to get married. They teased him about the female plants who longed to be near him, for any one of them would have been happy to be his wife.

The young Lali Guras, content with his quiet life spreading beauty in the forest, did not want to get married. 'Listen, my dear friends,' he said, 'everyone is happy with me. Look at the humans. Whenever I flower, they come here, marvel at me and go back happy. Let me live my life like this. What I need to do is flower for the gods every spring, spread happiness in the world and not think of anything else. Do not force me to move out of this sacred realm.'

This did not please his friends. 'This is no reason not to get married,' they retorted. But Lali Guras remained steadfast. The monsoons approached and the flowers in the forest started to fade away.

Worried that his best friend would have no one to take care of him during old age, Chaap, another species of plant growing at this altitude, enquired, 'Have you changed your mind?'

'No,' replied the young rhododendron.

Chaap convened a meeting of all the plants, including Lali Guras. Once again, the question was raised. The young rhododendron, incensed by the same query, left the meeting, embarrassing his best friend. Next morning, Lali Guras and Chaap met. 'Your leaving the meeting last night was hurtful,' said Chaap. 'But I have learnt the reason why you refrain from getting married. And as your best friend I have decided not to interfere further to make you change your mind.'

This roused Lali Guras's curiosity. 'What reason, apart from my desire to serve the gods and spread beauty in the world, do you know of for my refusal to get married?' he asked.

Seizing the opportunity, Chaap said, 'Dear friend, it's so sad that no one is willing to marry you. That is why you have decided to remain single, to protect yourself from rejection. And it's true, who would marry you? You are just a short, stumpy tree while other trees around you are taller and more handsome.'

Lali Guras was taken aback by his friend's words. Provoked, he replied, 'My dear friend, what you say is completely wrong. Mind you, if I really want to marry, there is no dearth of females ready to marry me. But I would like to say that I do not wish to marry anyone from my immediate environs. Instead, I will go to a lower altitude to find my life partner.' Chaap was happy, for this is what he had wanted for his best friend.

Autumn had set in. The marriage season was in full swing everywhere. The cool Himalayan wind brought the sounds of wedding celebrations from the human world too. The young rhododendron along with his old father ventured in search of a bride. Both father and son looked unattractive as their flowers had died. Further, at lower altitudes, their leaves turned pale due to the heat.

They crossed a thick forest of oaks. Here Lali Guras spotted a beautiful daughter of a Himalayan alder tree. Utis, as she was locally called, was tall and slim, with graceful leaves and boughs. Lali Guras fell in love with her. Swaying his heavy branches laden with pale leaves, he knelt down before Utis and said, 'You are my first love. I like you and want to propose marriage. I never wanted to marry but have now given in to my friends and neighbours. I only had one condition—that I would marry a girl from outside my abode. So, I have chosen you. Will you marry me?'

'I am happy and would consider myself fortunate to marry you. You look quite handsome and would make a perfect match for me. But first, you need to get permission from my old father,' replied Utis.

Father and son approached the girl's father. When they reached Utis's father, he swayed his leaves and asked, 'Howcome you are here amid the alder grove? Is everything well?' The concern and courtesy shown by Utis's father eased the conversation. 'Why have you come here? Is there anything I may help you with?' he asked.

The rhododendrons felt awkward. Their heavy leaves could not dance in the breeze like those of the alder trees. However, mustering some courage, the old rhododendron spoke up. 'Sir, I have come here for a personal reason. My son has attained the age to marry. I have also grown old and may soon die. This is the reason why I come here to ask for your daughter's hand for my son. If you agree, the best time for marriage would be now, in the autumn.'

On hearing the old rhododendron's request, the girl's father turned red with rage. He was so angry that he began to shake and shed all his leaves. 'I am not happy. Marriage is sacred and can be entered into only among families that are of equal standard to each other. It is impossible that a rhododendron and an alder tree marry. I am tall and handsome and my daughter is slim and beautiful. My branches are strong and straight and all my leaves are so light they can easily dance in the slightest breeze. I am no less than the mighty oak, fir and pine in this forest. How can someone like you, who is stumpy, hunchbacked, with broad and heavy leaves, come here asking for my daughter? Agreeing to your proposal would be a disgrace for me and my family. Henceforth, do not dream of my daughter. Go away! Leave immediately. Do not show me your faces again.'

The rhododendrons were disheartened by the scorn the alder tree had subjected them to. However, since they had come on a mission, Lali Guras, notwithstanding the criticism, wanted to make one last effort. 'Sir, would you allow your daughter to visit our grove during springtime? Just to have a look, nothing else,' he requested.

Thinking there was no harm in visiting the rhododendron forest, Utis's father said, 'I can see no reason to object to your request. But before I let my daughter visit you in the spring, promise me you will never again think of marrying my daughter.'

'That is a promise, sir,' replied the young rhododendron. And the father-son duo trekked up to their grove with a heavy heart.

The autumn and long winter months gave way to spring. The gardens filled once again with the fragrance of numerous flowers. The forests were full of music, with the buzzing of bees. The rhododendrons shed their pale leaves and grew fresh, green ones. Buds bloomed and the beautiful pinkish-red flowers covered them. How lovely the rhododendron forest was!

The alder tree had grown very old. He was almost naked; all his branches had shed their leaves. His weak, black branches were filled with ants. His eyes were covered with spiders' webs.

He had forgotten the promise he had made to the young rhododendron to send his daughter to visit his abode.

Lali Guras waited in vain for Utis. Spring would be over soon. Father and son decided to go to the alder grove once again. The old alder tree suddenly saw something beautiful coming towards him—a breathtaking galaxy of pink flowers. Birds chirped and bees and butterflies started to buzz in the grove. The old alder had never seen such a magnificent tree in his life. It took him a while to recognise the rhododendrons.

He realised he had disgraced himself when he had humiliated the rhododendrons last autumn without knowing anything about them. He was of course in no way comparable to the wonderful rhododendron, which had turned into a handsome, colourful tree at this time of the year, while he had grown old, weak and ant-ridden. He began to repent.

As the father-son duo neared, the old alder tree thought it better to die than face the humiliation of meeting them. A major landslide had occurred nearby. The old alder tree jumped into that landslide and died.

When Utis came to know what her father had done, she

ran to be near him. But when she saw the rhododendrons in full bloom, she could hardly take her eyes off them. The flowers of Lali Guras were so attractive that Utis instantly fell in love with him. She knew he was the one for her and without hesitation said, 'You look very handsome. Will you marry me?'

'O, my beautiful girl, there's no luck for us,' replied Lali Guras in distress. 'I have loved you all these days. As instructed by you, I even approached your father to ask for your hand in marriage, but he refused. He also made me promise that I would never think of marrying you.'

'How could my father refuse to marry me to such a handsome tree like you?' Utis cried in grief. She lingered around Lali Guras, trying to persuade him to marry her. But no amount of crying could weaken him. He was honest and did not want to break the promise he had made to Utis's father, even for love!

The rhododendron left for home without marrying Utis. But the young Utis was reluctant to be away from her lover and followed him up to his abode. Mesmerised by his beauty, she cursed herself for her ill luck.

The monsoons arrived. Persistent rains triggered a series of landslides. With no response from her lover, Utis, dejected at her fate, decided to go back to the grove of alder trees. On her way back, she jumped down a mountainside and was crushed in a landslide, just like her old father.

This is why alder trees are usually found in landslide-prone areas. And it is believed that whenever there is a landslide, an alder tree will fall down. When the Lepchas see the fallen alder tree, they repeat this love story.

References

1. The rhododendron (*Rhododendron niveum*) is Sikkim's state tree.

The Hare
and the
Old Couple

A long, long time ago, there lived an old couple in the Himalayas. Every spring morning, the old couple would climb up a forest path. With the help of two canes they would dig holes and drop seeds into the holes. The seeds later bore fruit and crops, enough to last the couple for a year. It was hard work, and the poor couple had no help, as they were childless.

One day, the old woman decided to stay back and finish household chores. Her husband set off into the forest. It was a sunny day. The sweet fragrance of flowers and the humming of bees announced the arrival of spring. A multitude of bees flew towards the old man and hovered over his head for a while. Oblivious to the good omen bees bring, the old man continued clearing the ground, when suddenly he found a newborn baby amid the shrubs. He rushed towards the sobbing baby and held him close to his bosom. 'Whose child is this? How did this child come to be in this dense forest? This must be godsent. I will take the baby to my wife. She will be very happy,' he said to himself and set off for home with the baby in his arms.

The old woman, busy preparing food, was surprised to see her husband return home so soon. And then she saw the baby in his arms. Shocked, she ran up to him and peered at the baby. Both sat around the hearth and cuddled the baby for a long time. They had never felt happier. From the next day, the old woman stayed home to look after the baby, and the old man went into the forest to sow the seeds.

Hearing the news of a newborn baby in a hut nearby, a hare hatched a plan to have a good meal. Unmindful of the scorching sun, he ventured out from his burrow and went to the old couple's house.

'Grandma, a large number of animals have entered your fields. They have started eating all your crops,' shouted the hare.

'Thank you for informing me. But since I have a newborn baby, and there is no one to look after him, would you mind chasing the animals away, my good son,' pleaded the old woman.

'Certainly. I'm happy to help you, Grandma,' said the hare.

A fortnight passed. The cunning hare hit upon another idea. 'Grandma, again animals are feeding on your crops,' said the hare, 'Go to the fields to chase them away while I look after your baby.' To be fair, since the hare had chased away the animals last time, the old woman agreed.

Out in the fields, the old woman surveyed the crops. There

were no signs of any animal. She dug up some carrots to give the hare. When she came back home, she was in for a big surprise. The hare greeted her at the door, his mouth greasy. 'Grandma, I have lulled your baby to sleep. I have also prepared some food for you and Grandpa. I am going back now,' the hare said, and without waiting to take the carrots the old woman had brought for him, he hopped back to his burrow.

The hare had not only cooked a meal, he had cleaned the house too! 'Mmmmmm, what an aroma!' the old woman thought, lifting the lid of the vessel that was bubbling on the stove. 'Is it chicken curry or is it lamb? From where did the hare get this wonderful meat?'

The old woman picked up a piece and put it in her mouth. 'So tasty!' she said to herself, 'Three score and ten years have I attained, but I have never cooked such a lovely dish in my life!'

Thinking of her baby, she went to the cradle to give him his evening supper. But then she decided to let him sleep while she finished her remaining chores. 'I'll wake up the baby when my husband returns. We can all enjoy our evening meal together,' she thought.

The old man returned home thoroughly exhausted. His wife was waiting to serve him the tasty dish. The couple fell upon the food. They ate with gusto. Satisfied, all they needed to do now was play with their baby awhile and then go to sleep.

While the aroma still lingered in the kitchen, the old woman went to bring the baby from his cradle. But where was the child? Twigs and branches and leaves had been arranged inside the cradle to make it look as if a baby was sleeping. For a while she stared stupidly at the cot.

And then the old couple's world came crashing down. 'Oh no! We've eaten the flesh of our very own child! How could we have done this?' cried the old woman. They realised the hare had tricked them. What was the couple to do now? 'My dear wife, do not worry. I will find the culprit, bring him to you and kill him in front of your eyes,' said the old man, anger surging in his heart.

Next morning, the old man began to sharpen his knife on a stone. 'How dare you kill my son! I will not leave you, come what may,' the old man said as he sheathed the knife and set off in search of the hare.

Crossing seven hills and seven rivers, the old man came upon Ri Mapuo or Red Mountain. Here, he spotted a red hare. 'I am looking for a hare that killed my baby. Have you seen him? Why are you red in colour?' the old man enquired.

'Grandpa, I have been feeding upon red grass and living on red soil and red mountains for many years now and thus I have turned red. I don't know about the hare that killed your baby,' the hare answered. The old man believed him and stroked the hare with the blunt side of his knife.

Taking shelter in a cave for the night, the old man ate some buckwheat bread, which his wife had packed for him. At daybreak he continued his search. He crossed several passes and streams to reach Ri Hampu or Green Mountain. Here the old man spotted a green hare. 'I am looking for a hare that killed my baby. Have you seen him? Why are you green in colour?' the old man enquired.

'I have been staying on green earth, consuming green grass and drinking green water and so I have turned green. I don't know about the hare that killed your baby,' replied the green hare. The old man believed him and stroked the green hare with the blunt side of his knife.

He now set off towards Ri Kapu or White Mountain. The path was covered in snow and the old man was beginning to feel very tired. At dusk he found a white hare licking his greasy lips. 'Why are your lips so oily? How have your lips turned so greasy?' the old man asked.

Not recognising the old man, the hare replied, 'Let me tell you a story. There was an old couple over there in the mountains. One day, the old man had gone to the fields leaving behind his wife and a child at home. I devised a plan and killed the baby and had a hearty meal.'

'You are the one who killed my baby,' the old man shouted. Dragging the hare into his bag, he set off for home.

By dawn he had reached the outskirts of his village. He decided to quench his thirst at the stream before going home. He slung the bag on a tree and bent down to drink. The hare got his chance to escape. Hopping out of the bag, he placed a stone inside it. Having quenched his thirst, the old man slung the bag across his shoulders and continued on his journey home.

The old woman was waiting for her husband's return. She had a pot of boiling water ready. The old couple had planned to throw the hare into the boiling water.

'I have got the hare who killed our baby. Is the water ready?' the old man asked.

The old woman opened the lid of the pot and the old man overturned his bag into the pot. The stone splashed into the water, burning the old woman. 'The hare has tricked me!' Seeing his wife injured, the old man was not in a state to forgive the cunning animal.

Next day, the old man set out again to look for the greasy-lipped hare. He was lucky this time; he spotted the hare within a few hours. He dragged the hare into the bag and took him home, not stopping on the way this time.

The sharp-witted hare saw a ladder in the kitchen leading to the attic. Afraid of being killed, the hare pleaded, 'Do not drop me in boiling water. If you really want to kill me, then use your bow and arrow. To make doubly sure you do kill me, let Grandma stand on top of the ladder with the grinding stone in her hands. Keep me in the middle and you shoot the arrow from below. If you miss, or I try to escape, Grandma can drop the grinding stone on me,' said the hare.

How foolish the couple were to trust the hare again!

No sooner had the old man shot an arrow, it directly hit the old woman at the top of the ladder, for the hare hopped away. The grinding stone, which the old woman was holding, fell upon the old man, and both of them died.

People living in the Himalayas remain wary of the hare, for he is a very shrewd and clever animal.

The Abominable Snowman

On a small farm in the middle of the great Himalayas there lived a middle-aged man named Atek. He was a herder, looking after scores of cattle, sheep and goats. Every evening, Atek would burn logs in front of his farm to keep himself warm and to drive wild animals away.

Atek's farm was very far from other settlements. All he could see from his house were snow-capped peaks and mountains covered with tall trees and plenty of grass. Alone in the forest, Atek would, after herding the animals, sit by the fireside and play soulful tunes on his *puntong palit*,[1] his only companion. This daily pastime had turned him into a refined flautist.

It was late afternoon one day. The

cattle were in the stables, their stomachs full after a day of grazing. Atek had almost finished all his chores, including milking the cows. Sitting beside the fire he had made in his front yard, he began to cut yams and other jungle vegetables for his evening meal. Putting the vegetables to boil in a pan over the fire, Atek took out his puntong palit and started playing. He had barely finished playing one tune, when his ears pricked up. He thought he heard leaves rustling. He strained to hear more, but all was quiet and still. Shaking his head, Atek resumed playing the flute. Again he heard the same rustling of leaves. As he craned his neck to see what was making the noise, he saw a tall, hirsute and aggressive-looking *jyamphi moong*.[2] The abominable snowman!

It was a female yeti for the herdsman could see two long, enormous breasts hanging from her chest. Atek trembled in fear but did not want to show it. From the corner of his eyes, he noticed her heels faced the front and the toes were backwards. Atek's heart started pounding. He knew that since female yetis are bigger and fiercer than the males, they mate only once a year during the mating season. As soon as they complete their mating, they go their own separate ways. Being in the forest for several years, the herdsman also knew that the creature seldom ventured out in the daytime but became aggressive at night.

Pretending he had not seen the yeti, Atek continued to play the flute. The music seemed to delight the yeti. Mesmerised by the tunes emanating from the flute, the female yeti came close to Atek and seemed to listen to the music with rapt concentration and interest. Soon Atek's hands grew tired and lips parched as a result of continuously playing the flute. He put down the instrument involuntarily, unmindful of the scary creature near him. It was time for him to go to sleep or he would be too tired to take the cattle out to graze the next morning. But as soon as he put the flute down, the yeti took one mighty leap towards the fire, picked up the flute and flung it back at Atek, signalling him to play it. Atek could feel his heart drumming and the hair on his hands stood up. The silence all around was great and awful. He had no other option but to do what the creature wanted him to do. He played his bamboo flute until dawn when the creature suddenly disappeared into the forest.

The next evening Atek intentionally did not play his flute hoping the yeti would not revisit him. To his disappointment, the yeti appeared, and picking up the flute, indicated Atek should play it. Atek was once again forced to play the flute until dawn.

The following evening, Atek collected more logs from the forest and made a big fire. Finishing his chores, he sat by the fire and took out his flute. This time, he played softly, a long, soothing tune that he had never played before. The forest echoed with the unusual sound. Even the animals at the ranch pricked up their ears. As usual, the yeti came and listened. Feeling parched, Atek placed the instrument on the ground, intending to take a break. This time the female yeti picked up the flute and instead of making Atek play it, she tried to play it herself. Sadly, the female yeti could not produce any sound from the flute. Once again, she placed the flute near Atek's lips, signalling him to play. Once again, he played until dawn when it was time for the yeti to go back to the forest.

This continued for several days. Atek's life became hell. The yeti would not allow him to rest and sleep. It was beyond his endurance. Tired and afraid, the herdsman knew fleeing from the creature and abandoning the ranch would be of no use. Instead, he hatched a plan to kill it.

The next evening, he built a big fire and instead of playing the flute, started to massage his whole body from head to foot with butter, sitting next to the fire. The herdsman had an inkling that the yeti would imitate him. To make sure his trick worked well, Atek kept plenty of butter with him.

As expected, the yeti arrived. Luckily, it was a full moon. Instead of coming close to Atek, the yeti stood at a distance and observed Atek applying butter and massaging his whole body from head to toe. Occasionally, Atek would stop applying the butter and play his flute to draw the yeti near him. It worked. The yeti came and stood close to the fire. Soon the yeti started to imitate Atek. She took a bit of butter and applied it on her body, massaging it in from head to foot as Atek was doing. Her body became brown and shiny and looked beautiful in the moonlight.

Atek waited for the right moment. After several instances of the yeti applying butter to her body, the clever herdsman took out a piece of firewood from the fire and pretended to rub it all over his body to warm himself. To his relief, the female yeti also picked up a piece of burning wood and rubbed it over herself. Her hirsute body immediately caught fire. Engulfed in flames, screeching in pain, the creature ran into the forest. The flames got bigger and bigger.

She came across a hunter, from whom she sought help to protect herself. 'Brother, help me!' the yeti cried out in pain. The hunter replied: 'If someone has set you on fire, jump into water, but if you have set yourself on fire, flee towards the snow-covered peaks of the upper Himalayas.'

The yeti knew that she had set herself on fire. So she ran towards the snow-covered peaks of the upper Himalayas never to return where humans were settled.

The Lepchas living in the foothills of the Himalayas and the Bhutias tending cattle in the forests believe the yeti still lives in the snow-covered high Himalayan mountains. They also believe that the yeti, influenced by Atek's music, usually whistles a long, haunting tune when it comes out early in the morning and at night in search of food. Whistling and playing the flute also attract a yeti—the reason why people refrain from whistling or playing the flute while travelling along the paths of the high, snowy mountains.

References

1. A four-holed flute made of bamboo.
2. Lepcha name for the yeti. Also known as *sokpa* in Nepali and *ajyo mighee* in the Bhutia dialect.

Khye Bumsa, the Wandering Prince

*I*n the early thirteenth century, a letter dropped from the heavens in a palace where three brothers lived as chiefs of Kham Minyak Andong.[1] Inscribed in gold, it urged the second prince to go south towards Bayul Demoshong, the hidden fruitful valley, present-day Sikkim, where his descendants would rule. Impelled by this divine command, Guru Tashi, the second brother, consulted the royal astrologer and on an auspicious date moved with his five sons.

He first proceeded to Lhasa, where he paid his respects to Jo Rinpoche or Lhasai Jo. 'Go towards the south-west. And there you will find a country called Demoshong,' the deity foretold. On their way, the royal entourage came to Sakya. Guru Tashi and his family decided to pay their respects to the king there.

The Sakyas at that time were constructing a seven-storey hall at Phurpa Lhagang monastery. The hall was to be supported by four immense wooden pillars and one hundred and sixty smaller ones. Several thousand workers had been trying to erect the pillars but had consistently failed in their attempts. Guru Tashi's eldest son came forward and displayed his enormous strength by erecting the pillars single-handedly. Since then he came to be known as Khye Bumsa, or the man with the strength of hundred thousand men. The young man did not win only this name, he also won the hand of the Sakya princess Jomo Gurumo.

Shortly thereafter, Guru Tashi's family left Sakya and moved to Pakshi, to the north-west of Khambajong. At Pakshi, Khye Bumsa built the Pakshi Gompa for four hundred monks. One of his brothers became a priest and lived there as the abbot. He built another monastery called Samdup Lhagang at Phari. Here, Guru Tashi died.

Khye Bumsa, following the sacred divination, continued his journey towards Demoshong, first proceeding to Khangbu Tahlung on the western branch of the Mochu river. At Khangbu, the prince met Shabdung Lhari, a high priest, who performed his father's last rites. Khye Bumsa then travelled further south, living for some time in Tromo Khang Chung and Chumoshong with his queen, and then came to Chumbi where he built a masonry house.

The prince, easily distinguishable from others as he was tall and well-built, had become quite popular because he was endowed with miraculous strength. Ngawang Gyadpai Palbar, an athlete unmatched in strength in Bhutan, heard the news that a man known as 'the one with the strength of a hundred thousand men' was living in Chumbi. 'I must go to Chumbi to see this man. How can this man take the title of the strongest man when I am still alive? I'll challenge him to a match to prove that I am the strongest man on earth,' thought Ngawang Palbar. Khye Bumsa was apprised that Palbar would be coming to Chumbi to challenge him to a duel. Not wishing to engage in unnecessary showcasing, Khye Bumsa yoked a pair of yaks and started working among others in the fields to avoid being noticed by Palbar.

It so happened that on nearing Chumbi, Palbar stopped at the fields where Khye Bumsa was working. He asked the men there, 'Hello, can you tell me where this man equalling the strength of a hundred thousand men lives in Chumbi?' 'This is the man who has come to challenge me,' the prince suspected, and not wanting to encounter Palbar, crossed with his yaks to the other side of the bridge. There he unyoked the animals, and lifting the plough and ploughshare with one hand placed it near a willow tree. Unknown to the prince, Palbar had witnessed this feat, and followed him to his house.

Being a good host, Khye Bumsa invited Palbar inside and treated him to tea and wine and a good dinner. Palbar challenged the prince to a wrestling match but the prince refused. On being repeatedly challenged, Khye Bumsa asked his wife to bring three containers of mustard seeds. 'Get me a bowl too,' he told his wife. With seeming ease, Khye Bumsa started pressing the mustard seeds with his bare hands and extracted oil. Palbar was anxious to show his strength and asked for a similar quantity of mustard seeds. 'Provide only one container of mustard seeds,' Khye Bumsa told his wife. To Palbar's chagrin, he could not produce a single drop of oil.

Provoked, for he had failed to produce oil from the mustard seeds, Palbar challenged Khye Bumsa to a trial of strength and asked him to walk out to the fields. Tired of Palbar's arrogance, Khye Bumsa agreed. Presenting his left hand to

Khye Bumsa, Palbar taunted him to hold tight for he was going to twirl the prince around on the strength of one arm. Khye Bumsa held on so tight that Palbar fell to the ground in pain and had to let go.

Now, it was Khye Bumsa's turn to offer his hand for Palbar to grasp. Khye Bumsa offered his right hand and held on to Palbar's extended arm with such firmness and strength that he wrenched it off Palbar's shoulder. Palbar was thrown five to six paces away. Such was Palbar's excitement that on being thrown he declared boastfully, 'Look, how strong I am! I am free of your grasp.' But the next moment, when Khye Bumsa held up the detached arm and said, 'Whose arm is this?' Palbar looked down and was shocked to find his arm torn from his shoulder.

Defeated, Palbar made his way back home.

∾

Three years had passed in Chumbi. Khye Bumsa still had no children to carry on his line. He grew concerned. Then he heard that in the interior of Demoshong, to the south-west of Chumbi, there lived a great Lepcha patriarch called Thekong Tek and his wife Nyo-kung Ngal who could confer the boon of progeny. After due consultation with his priests and a number of divinations, all of which promised success, Khye Bumsa resolved to pay a visit to the great Lepcha wizard.

The prince started the journey to Demoshong carrying various kinds of gifts. Crossing Yakla, the entourage reached Rangpo, the present-day border of Sikkim with the state of West Bengal. Here, when Khye Bumsa enquired where the Lepcha patriarch and his wife lived, the villagers pointed in the eastern direction. Proceeding towards present Gangtok, they came across a very old man and woman, their faces blackened from tilling their recently burnt field. Khye Bumsa asked the couple, 'Do you know where Thekong Tek and Nyo-kung Ngal live?' The couple could not help the prince, but offered to go in search while the prince's party took rest.

Suspecting the couple knew more than they chose to reveal, the prince followed them to a bamboo house. There he found an old man seated on a raised throne of bamboo, clad in a robe, adorned with the head of a fierce-looking animal, wearing a garland of teeth and claws of wild beasts interspersed with various shells. His wife was busily engaged in getting food and drink ready.

When the royal entourage reached the hut, Nyo-kung Ngal called them in and served them wine and food. Recognising the couple as the one he had met in the burnt fields, Khye Bumsa bowed with folded hands, placed the gifts he had brought all the way from Chumbi, and beseeched, 'O great patriarch, I come here seeking the boon of progeny.'

'Young prince, you shall be the father of three sons,' assured the patriarch. 'And one of your descendants will become the king of Sikkim.'

Soon after Khye Bumsa returned to Chumbi, Jomo Gurumo, his wife, conceived and gave birth to a son, followed by two more. After the third son was born to the royal couple, Khye Bumsa thought it was time to celebrate by offering a thanksgiving prayer to the local deities of Sikkim and also to Thekong Tek and Nyo-kung Ngal. He descended via Chola and arrived at the cave at the foot of the Dong-tsa-gong rock, near the hillside of Kyachung La. There the prince and his entourage were met by Thekong Tek and Nyo-kung Ngal, who had come up from Sikkim bringing various fruits. They performed the prayers together. That cave later came to be known as Brag-dtsan and the three sons of Khye Bumsa came to be known as the three Brag-dtsan-dar brothers.

Coming down to Ringchom, near present-day Kabi or Kavi in north Sikkim, Khye Bumsa along with his wife and three sons personally thanked Thekong Tek for granting the boon of progeny. This simple yet profound gesture coming from the royals of Chumbi warmed the Lepcha patriarch who pledged eternal friendship. This pledge of friendship was cemented by a ceremony in which several animals were sacrificed. Both the parties sat on the raw hides of the animals, entwined the entrails around their persons, and put their feet together in a vessel filled with blood, thus swearing blood brotherhood to each other. Invoking all of Sikkim's local spirits, Thekong Tek asked them to bear witness to this solemn contract, invoking blessings on those who would observe this faithfully and curses on those who would break this eternal contract between the two races, thereby binding the Lepchas and the Bhutias in an inseparable bond as brothers, which still exists today.

At the very moment of invoking the blessing, the chirps of thousands of birds and the buzzing of bees echoed in the sacred grove. As he looked up in the air, Thekong Tek's eyes caught the pure, white peaks of Kongchen Kongchlo and the patriarch appealed to the mountain deity to also bear witness to the pact of blood brotherhood. Till date, there are nine stones (depicting the nine persons who engaged in the blood brotherhood pact) on top of a hillock at Kabi and they face the peak of Kongchen Kongchlo.

Khye Bumsa went back to Chumbi. The palace at Chumbi became prosperous and his sons grew up with the passage of time. Khye Bumsa wanted to test the minds and attitudes of his three sons. He summoned his first son. 'Son, tell me, how do you wish to earn your livelihood?' His first-born replied, 'I would like to snatch and take away, by fair means or foul, other people's properties and possessions.' The king fumed, 'Get lost! You are not worthy and will be a *kya-wo-rab*, a first-rate ruffian.'

He then asked his second son the same question. The

second prince had no ambition at all. 'Father, I do not care to have any subjects or followers but would be happy to till my land and earn my livelihood.' Khye Bumsa was not amused with this answer. 'You will make a first-class *lang-mo-rab*, a farmer, and nothing else.' The eight Bhutia clans comprising Bonpo, Gonsarpa, Namtsangkor, Tagchungdar, Kartsopa, Gyontopa, Tsungyalpa and Dokhangpa are the descendants of Khye Bumsa's first two sons.

In despair, the king called for his youngest son. 'Son, what do you want to do in your future?'

'I want to protect my followers and employ them in services and rule over them as their chief,' replied the youngest son. Happy beyond measure, the king blessed him, saying, 'Excellent! You will be *mi-pon-rab*, a first-rate ruler of men. May you live long. May your line succeed to the promised kingdom after my death and inherit the royal name.'

The youngest prince also married a Sakya princess. She soon gave birth to a son at her natal home. This son was called Shangdarpo or he who would enhance the fortunes of his uncle. She gave birth to her second son on the tenth day of the seventh month of the lunar calendar, coinciding with a festive day held in honour of Guru Rinpoche, the patron saint. This son was called Tse-chu-darpo meaning glorious or lucky tenth day. The third son was born on Zha Nyma or Sunday, so he was called Nyima Gyalpo or the solar king. The fourth son was born on a day when a consecration ceremony was being performed on the occasion of the completion of an image of Guru Rinpoche. He was therefore named Guru Tashi.

These four sons were then collectively called the Tong-du-ru-zhi, meaning the four clans of a thousand each. Tong-du-ru-zhi then became the four principal Bhutia clans. Later, all the families of these four clans along with the Beb-tsen gyed family settled in present-day Gangtok. Of all these, Guru Tashi's family became pre-eminent and inherited the princely name. His descendant, Phuntsog Namgyal, was consecrated as the first *chogyal*[2] of Bayul Demoshong, later called Sukhim or happy house, and now known to the outside world as Sikkim.

References

1. Kham Minyak Andong was situated to the west of Ta-tsien between Litang and Dirge in eastern Tibet.
2. Dharma king.

The Lake that Shifted

There are four hundred and four sacred lakes in Sikkim. Buddhists believe these holy lakes are the sacred abodes of different deities and *tsomens* or water nymphs. These deities are sanctified and worshipped to bring peace and prosperity to the people and the land. The most popular of the sacred lakes is Lobding Tso. As per legend it was located at Yuksam, where Phuntsog Namgyal was consecrated as the first chogyal of Sikkim. It is revered by everyone as the mother of all the sacred lakes since it is believed to be the abode of Pemachen Tsomen, the mother goddess of all water nymphs. Today it is called Khechoedpalri lake, located just below Khechoedpalri monastery, near Pelling in west Sikkim.

In the mid-seventeenth century,

Sikkim was ruled by the Namgyal dynasty. The kingdom was under constant attack from foreign invaders. War had broken out between the kingdom of Sikkim and neighbouring Nepal. The palace at Rabdentse was not very far from Lobding Tso. In the course of the fierce battle that ensued, a large number of humans and animals were killed. The lake was defiled with their dead bodies.

Near the lake there lived a hermit-monk on a secluded hilltop called Drubdi.[1] He had chosen this faraway spot as he did not want to be disturbed. No one dared go up the hill, except occasionally to offer prayers. The hermit-monk would spend six months in meditation without eating anything. During this period, he would go down the hill every morning for a jar of water from the sacred lake. He used the water to make offerings to the gods before starting his meditation. He had attained great spiritual powers but had not yet been blessed by the divine vision of Pemachen Tsomen.

One morning, the hermit-monk came down the hill as usual to take a jar of water. There was a kind of hush all around the lake. He could feel a divine presence. Standing still, he stared at the middle of the lake, which shone as if the sun had entered it. And lo! Pemachen Tsomen was revealed to him in all her majestic brightness. Awed, the hermit-monk knelt down, closed his eyes and offered prayers in respect. His one remaining wish of seeing the water goddess had been granted!

When he opened his eyes, the goddess was still there. This was surprising. The goddess asked for his help for she was disturbed by the massive pollution inside her abode. 'O man of good deeds,' the water nymph pleaded, 'will you help me shift to a cleaner location? I cannot live here any longer. I may soon die if I continue to stay here.' Saying these words, she disappeared.

The monk, a tantric master, immediately performed some prayers and began to move the lake. He found a peaceful site in the middle of the forest near Khechoedpalri. The area was serene, calm and clean—perfect for the water goddess to make her abode. He chanted prayers in praise of the water nymph, ending with '*Tso-shug*,' meaning 'Lake, please sit here.' Lobding Tso now came to be known as Tso-shug. But when the villagers began to frequent the lake and pollute the water, Pemachen Tsomen once again began to feel uncomfortable and wanted to shift.

One sunny day, making a sound of the hum of a thousand bees, the water nymph got out of the lake and shifted the lake uphill, where it sits at present. There, with the blue sky and a pleasant wind, everything was beautiful. The villagers had never before heard such a sound produced by the lake. It was so loud that they left their work in the forests and fields and hurried towards where the sound came from. When they reached the lake, they were shocked to see it had already shifted to a higher location. Only a puddle remained, which can be seen even today. From that day onward, the villagers refrained from defiling the lake and began instead to offer their prayers to the water goddess.

Devotees from far and wide visit Khechoedpalri lake once a year to perform special prayers, especially in the month of February (on the fifteenth day or full moon of the first Buddhist month), for fulfilment of their wishes. Prayers are usually offered at the small cavern at the source of the lake. They believe in the presence of Pemachen Tsomen in the lake because despite being surrounded by thick forests there is never a single leaf or twig in the serene, clear waters of the lake. They also believe that there is a pair of white swans that picks up every twig or leaf that falls in the water.

References

1. This is the hermitage of Gyalwa Lhabtsun Chennpo, one of the three pioneer lamas of Sikkim, now considered the first monastery of Sikkim.

How Humans were Saved from Demons

Once upon a time, there lived a poor young widow with her three daughters in a small hut. Despite being alone and having to take care of her children, she did not need to work hard. For she had a red-coloured cow, Lalmoo, which gave her everything— milk for the children and dung for the vegetables she cultivated in the fields. Every day, after completing her household chores, she would take the cow to graze in the nearby jungle, leaving her three children at home.

A demon named Simpindi had been destroying the world, hunting humans for their blood. Almost all humans on earth had been killed. The only survivors left were the widow and her three daughters. Simpindi sensed that there were still a few humans surviving in the world. 'I must destroy them,' the demon said to herself. Using her magical powers, she made her way to the widow's hut. The demon knew that the red cow was the reason for their survival. All she had to do was get rid of the cow.

The next day the cow got lost while grazing in the fields. The widow began searching for the cow everywhere. Her search led her into a dense forest. Wandering, she reached the heart of the forest. She grew afraid and said to herself, 'It's very dark here. My cow would never have ventured this far. I don't think I should continue.' But the thought of going back home without her cow was even more frightening. How would her family survive without the cow? So the poor widow silently continued down the forest path. She crossed a log bridge. 'Lalmoo! Lalmoo! Where are you? Come to me.' Her voice echoed back eerily in the silence among the trees. The sounds of the forest grew louder. She tensed. Then she laughed when she realised it was water falling from the branches of a tree.

Dark clouds had gathered around the afternoon sun. After walking for some more time, she saw smoke rising from a hut. When she looked closely, she saw the hut was similar to hers. An old woman sat in front combing her long, grey hair. The widow thought the old woman might have seen her cow. 'Anyo,' the widow called from the path above the hut, 'I am looking for my cow. Have you seen a red cow come here?'

'No, I haven't. But you seem tired. Come and have a cup of tea and then I will help you look for your lost cow,' said the old woman. Touched by the old woman's concern, the widow came down to the hut; after all, she was alone and tired and needed to rest awhile.

The old woman was pleased. Her plan had worked—she

was none other than Simpindi. Inside the hut, the old woman offered the widow a cup of tea along with a plate of fried meat. 'The fried meat tastes good. Eat it slowly. I have to go out on an urgent errand,' said the old woman.

'Okay, but hurry back. I can't stay here for long. I have to find my cow,' replied the widow.

The moment the demon stepped out of the house, the old woman's pet cat, wanting some of the meat, approached the widow and mewed, '*Miew, Miew, Sha khamchey chi phin nee chiek tik chi laou, Miew Miew* (If you give me a piece of meat, I will divulge a secret).' The widow was in no mood to share the meat for she was very hungry. 'Shoo . . . Shoo . . . go away. Can't you see I'm tired and hungry?' she chased the cat away.

With the cat chased away, the demon's pet dog came near the table and barked, '*Khow, Khow, Sha khamchey chi phin nee chiek tik chi laou, Khow, Khow.*' The widow chased away the dog too.

Just as she finished eating the meat, her head began to reel, and she fell unconscious. The plate of fried meat she had just eaten was of her red cow. Nor had the widow known that the cat and the dog were gods who had taken the form of the demon's pet animals to help her and tell her about the demon's trickery.

The sun had set. The demon came back, fully recharged, as demons usually tend to become after sunset. Seeing the unconscious widow, the demon tied a grinding stone on a rope, and pulling with all her might, dropped it on the widow's head, killing her instantly. She then relished the meat and the fresh blood dripping from the widow's body. The demon was now even stronger and determined to finish the human race. 'There are only three little girls on earth. I will soon eat them up,' she pronounced.

Back at the widow's hut, her three daughters began to worry, for neither their mother nor their cow had come back.

The eldest daughter decided to go and look for their mother. 'Sisters, you take care of the house. I'll go out to see where our mother has gone,' she said to her two younger sisters.

Following the same path taken by her mother, she set off in search of her mother and the red cow. Similarly, after a long walk in the dense forest, she saw an old woman in front of a hut. Oblivious of the misfortune that had befallen her mother and the red cow, the eldest daughter was very happy to see someone like a grandmother in such a desolate place. 'Anyo, have you seen my mother and a red cow? Did they pass by here?' she asked the old woman.

'No, young girl. But don't you worry,' the old woman answered. 'Your mother and the red cow may be around. You look so tired. Why don't you come down and begin your search after having a cup of tea with me?' The girl was tired and hungry, and she was grateful for the invite. She entered the old woman's hut. Alas, she met with the same fate.

Next day, the second sister went in search of her mother, her older sister and the red cow and the same fate came upon her. Now, only the youngest daughter survived, the lone human in the world. She was terrified but had to leave her house to find her lost mother, two older sisters and the red cow. 'I don't know where my mother and sisters have gone. It's been several days and none of them has returned with the red cow. Perhaps they are stuck in a landslide or are in trouble. I should go and look for them,' the youngest daughter said to herself.

Mustering courage, she proceeded towards the forest. Like her mother and sisters, after travelling for several hours, she came across an old woman in front of a hut. 'Anyo,' she cried out to the old woman, 'have you seen my mother and my two older sisters around here? They had gone out in search of our lost cow. I am worried for they haven't come home in several days. Can you help me?'

The demon knew that this youngest girl was the only human surviving in the world. 'O my sweet child,' said the old woman, 'I haven't seen your mother, older sisters and the red cow. Maybe your loved ones are lost in the dense forest. Maybe wild animals have attacked them. But don't you worry, dear. What's the use of your grandmother if she cannot help you trace your loved ones? Come down here and have a cup of tea. You look very tired.'

The young girl was offered tea and fresh meat similar to her mother and sisters. 'Drink your tea and have the meat. I will be back soon and will then help you find your loved ones,' said the old woman and left.

In despair, the young girl had lost her appetite for everything. She was in no mood to even sip the tea. She sat lost in her own thoughts. The cat and dog appeared and made their lyrical appeal: '*Sha khamchey chi phin nee chiek tik chi laou, Miew, Miew, Khow, Khow.*' Both animals kept repeating their plea.

The little girl was finally roused from her thoughts. 'Poor animals, they must be hungry. I don't feel like eating the meat. I'm in no mood to drink the tea. I will give them the meat. But what is it that they want to tell me?' she thought.

She reached for the plate and called the animals near her. 'Come and have this meat. Both of you can relish this,' she told them.

No sooner had the animals eaten a piece of meat, they divulged the secret. 'Do not stay here. The old woman is a demon. She is about to return. When she comes back, she will kill you. She is the one who killed the red cow, your mother and two sisters. You are the only human surviving in this world. If you don't run away from here, there will be no trace of human beings left. The demons will rule. So better run away and save the human world, my dear.'

'How can I run away from here? I am so young and my

tired legs cannot carry me further. I have walked all day to reach here. I need to rest. If she is a demon, she must be very powerful and will easily be able to catch me,' she told the animals in dismay.

'Run away,' directed the cat and the dog. 'And don't worry about anything. We will help you. We have taken the forms of a cat and a dog to save the human world. Here are three magic items—a *kyasey* (comb), a piece of charcoal and a white stone—to ward off the demon. Now listen carefully. We are going to tell you what to do with these items. Place the kyasey on the spot when you cross the first mountain. After crossing the second mountain, place the piece of charcoal, and place the white stone after crossing the third mountain. Across a big river near the fourth mountain, is where your great-great grandfather lives. He may be of some help to you. But it is very difficult to cross that river. If you cannot cross this river, you will have to seek help from your ancestor on the top of that fourth mountain. Hurry up and leave. Remember, follow our instructions. Good luck!'

The girl hastened to leave. As she crossed the first mountain, she placed the kyasey and moved on. The demon was already behind her. When the girl was about to reach the second mountain, the demon reached the first mountain. Because of her long, unkempt hair covering both her eyes, the demon did not see the kyasey and stepped on it. It immediately turned into countless thorns which pricked her feet. The demon had to sit down and remove all the thorns. There were so many thorns that it took her a long time.

This gave the young girl time to cross the second mountain where she placed the piece of charcoal. When the demon stepped on the charcoal, it turned into fire, engulfing the entire mountain. The demon could not walk through the fire and had to wait till it subsided. Soon the girl had crossed the third mountain. She had placed the white stone there and proceeded towards the big river. As soon as the demon reached the third mountain, the stone transformed itself into a huge mountain. But the demon was so powerful that she could scale the mountain with ease.

The young girl grew afraid. Moreover, her small legs were very, very tired. The little girl wanted help to get across the river and save herself from the demon. The girl sat down. Knowing that the demon would soon pounce upon her, the girl made a lyrical plea to her ancestor: '*Jhyo-jhyo, Jhyo-jhyo, Dhentha ma tha chyatha ta na, Jhyo-jhyo, Jhyo-jhyo* (Great-great grandfather, please send me an iron rope and not a rope made from millet dough, Great-great grandfather).'

A sound as loud as the surging river came from the other direction, '*Gaoley lothon yaa* (Wait, I'm just rising from my bed).'

The girl cried out in distress again, '*Jhyo-jhyo, Jhyo-jhyo, Dhentha ma tha chyatha ta na, Jhyo-jhyo, Jhyo-jhyo.*'

A sound as loud as the river came from the other side, '*Kera chingdo yaa* (I'm tying my belt).'

The third time, she said, '*Jhyo-jhyo, Jhyo-jhyo, Dhentha ma tha chyatha ta na, lha phidey gyapley Simpindi haondo, Jhyo-jhyo, Jhyo-jhyo* (Great-great grandfather, please send me an iron rope and not a rope made from millet dough. Simpindi the demon is just behind this mountain).'

Hearing that the demon was just behind her, Jhyo-jhyo jumped up and sent an iron rope to the girl. The girl clasped the rope and crossed the river safely, reaching the top of the mountain.

The demon, who had heard the girl pleading with her ancestor, also made a similar plea. Imitating the little girl, Simpindi made her appeal: '*Jhyo-jhyo, Jhyo-jhyo, Chyatha ma tha dhentha ta na, lha phidey gyapley Simpindi haondo, Jhyo-jhyo, Jhyo-jhyo.*' But instead of an iron rope, Simpindi asked for a rope made of millet dough.

Jhyo-jhyo sent Simpindi the demon a millet-dough rope. The demon clasped it but when she attempted to pull herself across the river, the rope broke and the demon fell into the surging waters below, never to come back. And from the last little girl, the human race survived.

The Mystical Vase

The foundation of a Buddhist monastery was being laid at Samye in central Tibet in the middle of the eighth century. Chogyal[1] Trisong Detsen, king of Tibet, had called Shantarakshita, an Indian tantric master, to complete the task. This provoked the local spirits, who embarked on a campaign of disasters—disease, floods, storms, hail, famines and drought. At night, they dismantled all the construction work done during the day. There seemed no end to the chogyal's worries.

Giving up all hope, Shantarakshita sought an audience with the chogyal. 'O righteous ruler of Tibet, there is a person by the name of Padmasambhava[2] in India. He is the greatest tantric master of all time. Send your people to bring him here. Only then will Samye monastery see the light of day,' Shantarakshita advised. The chogyal despatched envoys to bring Padmasambhava to the snow-covered Tibetan highlands.

With his prescience, Padmasambhava—today revered in Sikkim as Guru Rinpoche,[3] or the precious master—already knew of the chogyal's mission and met the royal entourage at Mangyul, somewhere between Nepal and Tibet. Legend has it that Padmasambhava was over a thousand years old then. On the way to Tibet, he began to subjugate the local spirits and made them take oaths to protect the dharma and its followers. He met Chogyal Trisong Detsen at Tamarisk forest at Red Rock and then went to the top of Mount Hepori where he brought all the gods and demons of Tibet under his command. Glorious Samye was then built without any hindrance, and completed within five years, consecrated by Padmasambhava and Shantarakshita amidst miraculous and auspicious signs.

There then began an extraordinary wave of spiritual activity in Tibet. It was during this time Padmasambhava performed a sacred ceremony dedicated to Avalokitesvara, the Lord of Compassion, on the behest of the chogyal and his devout followers. In the middle of this ceremony, to everyone's surprise, a protective deity called Damchen Dorje Lekpa appeared and offered a precious vase to Padmasambhava. Holding it in his hands, he filled it with some water and consecrated it with prayers, which continued for seven days. On the seventh day, when the tantric master made to close the vase, he sighted a miraculous occurrence. His meditation had been so powerful that the Lord of Compassion himself and his entire retinue of innumerable buddhas and bodhisattvas appeared in the air, whirled around the vase like bees hovering around flowers and immersed themselves in the water contained in the vase. The miracle did not end here. Inside the vase, the water boiled violently, triggering a huge earthquake, after which five coloured aura rays radiated from the vase and flashed up in different directions. How happy the precious master was! With great satisfaction, Padmasambhava began to chant prayers. Happy with Padmasambhava's virtuous deeds, the gods from the heavens sent down a shower of flowers and songs in praise of the tantric saint.

Padmasambhava then shared the sacred water with all the devotees and followers present there. As people sipped a drop of this water, they were cured of their illnesses. Some regained their eyesight. Many felt a soothing peace in their minds as if they were in deep meditation.

Later, the master toured the country to find an appropriate place to hide the holy vase. Subduing the demons in a cave in Tibet, Padmasambhava concealed the holy vase in the form of *ter*[4] for future practitioners. 'Here shall I lay this sacred urn. I entrust you with this vase until a spiritual man comes and reveals it for the sake of the fortunate beings of the earth,' instructed the master to the guardian demon of the cave.

True to his words, many centuries later, a boy was born, who later came to be known as Terton Gharwang Shigpo Lingpa, regarded as one of the famous treasure finders in Tibet. He foresaw the appropriate time to reveal the sacred vase for the benefit of the fortunate beings of that era. He formally unearthed the vase from the cave to the chanting of prayers and mantras, meditating on the Lord of Compassion, similar to what Padmasambhava had done centuries earlier. Later, he handed it over to another revered lama called Chogyal Takshamchen, who imparted its blessings to devotees and kept it under his custody for many years.

Later, Chogyal Takshamchen thought that the 'dark age'

was casting its shadow over Tibet and it was no longer safe to keep the sacred vase in Tibet. After much deliberation, he decided to hand it over to his trusted disciple Lama Ngadak Sempa Chhenpo. Lama Ngadak had plans to go to the hidden land of Bayul Demoshong. He was one among the three lamas who met at Yuksam[5] and consecrated Phuntsog Namgyal as the first chogyal of Sikkim. Takshamchen thought the vase would be safe there. And this was how the sacred vase was brought to Sikkim in the seventeenth century.

One spring morning, the sound of clarinets at Lhagang Marpo[6] in Yuksam were heard at an unusual hour. In the forests and fields, people hearing the sound left their work and hurried towards the shrine. Lama Ngadak was the master of Lhagang Marpo. After completing his meditation on a deity called Vajrakilaya in eastern Nepal, he had returned to Yuksam to conduct the Bhum Chu ceremony. Inside the shrine, devotees led by Lama Ngadak had been chanting mantras—*Om Mani Padme Hung Rhi*[7]—to the Lord of Compassion. The monks began to play the clarinets while Ngadak Lama rang his precious bell as unusual signs began to appear from a vase of water when the chanting of the sacred mantras crossed one billion chants. The water from the mystical vase began to emanate a sweet fragrance, filling the air for a long time—this had occurred when Guru Padmasambhava had performed the ceremony in Tibet.

Lama Ngadak continued the second ceremony at Rinchenpong in present-day west Sikkim and the third one in Barphung in south Sikkim. The fourth and fifth ceremonies were held at Tashiding. During each Bhum Chu ceremony, one billion mantras to the Lord of Compassion were recited to aggregate the blessings.

Later, when Ngadak Sempa Chhenpo shifted his seat from Yuksam to Tashiding, he built Jhampa Lhagang, the temple of Maitriya Buddha or future Buddha in 1651. In the sanctum sanctorum, he deposited the Bhum Chu vase. However, in the course of time, the monastery was rebuilt and the vase is today secure inside the shrine room of the main monastery.

The Bhum Chu ceremony, when mantras to the Lord of Compassion are chanted, then became an annual feature in Tashiding monastery. Every year on the fourteenth day of the first Buddhist month (Tshepa Chuzhi), which falls sometime between February and March, hundreds trek up to Tashiding monastery, braving the arduous climb, rain and chill to witness the ceremony. The festival has reached its zenith of popularity and attracts not only Buddhists but followers of other faiths as well.

The opening of the ceremony is a solemn occasion. With the simultaneous rendition of clarinets and other tantric instruments, at midnight on the night of the full moon, the room containing the vase is unlocked under the observation of the *kutchab*[8] deputed from the state ecclesiastical department on behalf of the government. The vase contains twenty-one cups of water, which is measured every year in the presence of the kutchab to examine its quantity and quality. Each sign has its own significance indicating a good or bad omen. As per customary belief, if the water is found to be less than twenty-one cups, it signifies famine and drought; if it is more than twenty-one cups, it signifies floods and landslides. Clear water signifies peace while murky water means epidemics, unrest or war. The kutchab carefully records the quantity and quality of the water and the ecclesiastical department, in consultation with high incarnate lamas, performs remedial rites or *shabrim* to defuse the bad omens.

Since the commencement of the first Bhum Chu ceremony, the water for refilling the pot is always collected from Rathong Chu—the river which receives the tributaries of many sacred lakes and streams of the high mountains which were sanctified by the precious master. Modern studies show that the water from Rathong Chu is very pure and rich in healthy minerals.

The Sikkimese believe that anyone who drinks a drop of Bhum Chu water can cleanse themselves from the bad karma of past lives and will not go to hell. Also, those who drink this holy water are always protected by Lord Avalokitesvara and will be reborn in the blissful realm of the Lord of Compassion.

They say that many miraculous events still occur when monks open the sacred vase every year. It usually rains that night; the belief is that it cleans the surroundings for the ceremony. It is also said that the inside of the vase, covered with traditional silk scarves, is clean, fresh and germ-free, though it has remained unwashed and been kept away from the sun since the eighth century. Water produced in the eighth century is still there, clear and emitting the sweet fragrance it did all those centuries earlier.

References

1. Dharma king.
2. Lotus-born.
3. Also revered as the patron saint of Sikkim.
4. Sacred relics.
5. Meeting place of the three lamas who 'discovered' Sikkim as Bayul Demoshong, or the hidden fruitful valley.
6. Literally, red shrine.
7. Six-syllable mantra to Avalokitesvara, the Lord of Compassion, encompassing six realms which when chanted helps in the deliverance of all sentient beings of the six realms from suffering.
8. Representative.

Lapcha Dem, the Rock Fairy

*O*nce upon a time, there lived an old couple who had two children—a quick-tempered son and a kind-hearted daughter. When the son grew up, his parents got him married and soon they had a grandson.

One day, the newborn baby suddenly fell ill. When the baby did not get better, the family consulted a local shaman. The old shaman revealed that the cause of the child's illness was the presence of Lapcha Dem, the daughter of the house. 'If you want the newborn child to survive in this house, you should kill Lapcha Dem or keep her away from the house, far away in a forest cave,' cautioned the shaman.

Deep inside their hearts, Lapcha Dem's parents did not want their daughter to be killed or abandoned, nor could they ignore the shaman's warning. Their ill-tempered son, believing the shaman's divination and devoid of any love towards his sister, dragged her and left her in a cave very far from the house, all alone. There was no one to feed her or look after her. Back home, the shaman's prediction seemed to have worked. The baby recovered.

In a distant village, there lived a kind man who used to tend flocks of sheep. One afternoon, as the shepherd was returning home, his ears picked up what sounded like the cries of a child. He looked around but could not see anyone. The cries did not cease. He thought they came from the direction of the rock cave. When the shepherd went inside the cave, he spotted a young girl who looked like a fairy. She was Lapcha Dem, the rock fairy. He took pity on the child and took her to his house. She grew up to be a beautiful woman. The shepherd then married her.

They led a peaceful life. The shepherd tended his flocks while Lapcha Dem looked after the house and prepared delicious food for him every day. She would spend her time singing soulful songs, waiting for her husband to return home in the evening. She had no one to call her own save her husband, who loved her more than anything in the world.

One day, while she was in the middle of a beautiful song, her mother happened to pass by the shepherd's village. 'Is this my daughter's voice? The wind is bringing a message from my daughter . . . Is she alive? Where is she? How is she?' the mother wondered. When she reached home, the old lady told her husband and son, 'Today I heard our daughter's voice near a forest. She was singing a very beautiful song. I trust my ears. I am sure our Lapcha Dem is alive.'

The father sneered, 'Stop that. How can you think our daughter is alive after so many years? She's dead. Forget all this nonsense.'

The next morning, without telling anyone in the house about her decision to meet her daughter, the old woman proceeded in the direction of the village where she had heard her daughter singing. She found a beautiful girl in front of a hut singing a song. 'This is Lapcha Dem. I must take her back home,' thought the mother. She sang to her daughter, '*Amey phum Lapcha Dem, ama nyampu jhugey* (Mother's beloved daughter, Lapcha Dem, come with your mother. Let's go back home).' Lapcha Dem replied in a lyrical tone, '*Chungdi ama mepay, bomdi ama mingo, Michnag kyongi nanglo khada kapu laso* (There was no mother when young, I don't need one when grown up. It is strange, all are welcoming me now).'

Ashamed and bitter, the mother went away, sobbing all the way home. She narrated the incident to her husband. 'Our daughter Lapcha Dem is alive and living in a distant village in a shepherd's home. She's grown up and is very pretty. She's married to that shepherd and has been looking after his house. She was singing a very beautiful song while I was there. I asked her to come back home with me, but she refused.'

On hearing this, the father also wanted to bring his daughter home. The next morning, without saying a word to his wife or son, he took some paddy as a gift and rushed towards the shepherd's house. The father made a lyrical plea to his daughter: '*Apey phum Lapcha Dem, apo nyampu jhugey* (Father's beloved daughter, Lapcha Dem, come with your father. Let's go back home together).' In her sweet voice, Lapcha Dem replied, '*Chungdi apo mepay, bomdi apo mingo, michnag kyongi nanglo khada kapu laso* (There was no father when young, I don't need one when grown up. It is strange, all are welcoming me now).' Feeling guilty, the father went back home, sobbing all the way.

The old couple persuaded their son to go and get Lapcha

Dem home. When he reached the shepherd's house, he harshly asked her to come with him. Lapcha Dem gave him the same answer she had given her parents. Hot-headed as usual, not in the mood to listen, he dragged Lapcha Dem home.

At dusk, when the shepherd returned, he was greeted by an empty hut. There was no fire in the hearth and no meal on the table. He looked for his wife everywhere, in the house and in the cave, but could not find her. 'Where has my wife gone?' he brooded with a heavy heart. Hoping his wife would return soon, the shepherd proceeded to milk the sheep. All of a sudden a crow alighted near him and dropped a letter, saying, 'Your wife Lapcha Dem has sent this letter to you.'

Delighted, the shepherd read the letter. 'Beloved, as soon as you read this letter, do come to my parents' house. My cruel brother has forcibly taken me. Come soon, do not delay.' Without a moment's delay, the shepherd rushed towards his wife's natal home. When he reached there, he saw his wife sitting with her parents and sister-in-law. Her brother was sharpening a long knife nearby.

Looking unconcerned, but feeling apprehensive, the shepherd greeted his wife's parents. They welcomed him to their home and asked him to stay the night. He waited for the opportune moment to speak with his wife privately. That night, when everyone had fallen asleep, he went to Lapcha Dem's bed, gently shook her awake, and asked, 'Dear, why was your brother sharpening that long knife?'

She replied, 'My cruel brother has plans to kill you. But I will never let that happen. I will die in your place. Listen carefully. You sleep in my bed and I will sleep in yours. My cruel brother will kill me believing that it is you. No one will be able to lift up my corpse, except you. You must adorn my coffin with lotus flowers and silk scarves and take it to the crematorium. While I am being cremated, walk through the smoke and follow me. Only if you do exactly what I have told you, will we meet again.'

The shepherd promised to follow her instructions.

As predicted by Lapcha Dem, the cruel brother made his way stealthily to the shepherd's bed and slit his sister's neck, killing her instantly. Next morning, seeing his dead sister, the brother cried out. With tears in his eyes and a heart full of regret, he prepared a coffin for his dead sister. But when he tried to lift the body to put it inside, it was so heavy that he could not move it. Everyone in the village tried to lift the corpse together but to no avail. Finally, the wicked brother went to the shepherd, knelt before him and pleaded: 'Look, I will not beat you. I will not kill you. I request you to help us put my sister's corpse inside the coffin and carry it to the crematorium.'

This was as the rock fairy had predicted. To everyone's surprise, the shepherd lifted the corpse without any difficulty. He decorated the coffin exactly as his wife had asked him to. As the corpse burnt, the shepherd sat on a stone bewailing his loss. Suddenly, he remembered Lapcha Dem's last instruction—to follow her by walking through the smoke. Wiping his tears, he walked through the smoke, until it twirled him, bringing him beside a spring. As he gazed at the spring, a young boy emerged to fetch some water. The shepherd then spotted a hut on a hill. The boy too had spotted the man and rushed home to the hut to inform his sister. 'Sister, I saw a man at the spring.' She replied, 'Oh brother, bring him here quickly, right now.'

The hut and the spring were nothing but heaven and the girl inside the hut was the rock fairy. When the boy brought the shepherd to the hut, he recognised the fairy to be his wife. The girl too recognised her husband from her former life. The fairy then took the shepherd with her to heaven and they lived happily ever after.

Namsamay and His Magic Drum

One hot, sultry day, Khappura Nellongdimma Teegenjonga was alone in a hut set amidst high mountains. Thinking of her bad deeds towards her brother, which had made him abandon home, she began to weep. 'It's time I look for my brother and seek his forgiveness. Come what may, I will bring him back home,' she thought. Soon, Khappura set out in search of Kesingen, her only brother.

Days of walking led her into a deep forest. She was terribly thirsty, and looked around for some water or any wild fruit to quench her thirst. She came upon a huge, flat rock. Tired, she lay down on the rock. Lying there, Khappura regained some strength. When she opened her eyes, she found herself breathing in the cool forest air. From the corner of her eyes she spotted two small ponds on either side of the rock. 'This is amazing! Just a moment ago there was no trace of water but now there are two ponds! I hope this is not an illusion.' Khappura jumped off the rock and ran to the ponds. She drank to her heart's content. Then she resumed her journey, her stomach full of water as if it would suffice for a lifetime.

After several days of fruitless search, Khappura reached Munakham, somewhere in eastern Tibet. Here, agonised by her brother's loss, she made up her mind never to return home but to settle down in the midst of the forests surrounding Munakham. She constructed a small hut on the banks of a river and started to live there alone, engaging herself in weaving. Thoughts of her brother still kept plaguing her. One night, she heard a loud voice in her dream. 'Listen carefully, O young woman. This is the voice of God. You have conceived. You mistook the water in the ponds as rain water and drank it. The water on the left side of the flat rock was a tiger's urine while on the right side was your brother's urine. Since you have drunk water from both the ponds, you will give birth to twins—one will be a tiger and the other a human baby.' Startled, Khappura got up, shivering with fear.

Weeks after this frightening dream, Khappura began to experience birth pangs. As pronounced by the voice in her dream, she gave birth to twins and named them Kesamay and Namsamay.

When the twins grew up, they became interested in hunting wild animals and birds. In due course of time, hunting became their favourite pastime as well as their means of livelihood. Kesamay, whose heart was that of a tiger, always hunted for poisonous creatures like snakes, crabs, frogs, toads, scorpions and lizards. Namsamay, with the heart of a man, hunted for deer, bear, rabbit, stags and birds.

Bothered by his brother's inclination towards killing poisonous creatures, Namsamay suggested, 'Brother, why don't you stop hunting for poisonous creatures. It is quite dangerous. Instead, why don't you join me and hunt for birds and deer?'

'Mind your own business or else I will kill you and eat you up,' Kesamay retorted. After that day, relations between the two brothers turned sour. Kesamay became vengeful and wanted to kill his brother.

Taken aback by Kesamay's sudden change in behaviour, Namsamay went to his mother and told her about his fears. 'Don't worry, son,' Khappura comforted. 'I will protect you from Kesamay.' From that day onwards, whenever Kesamay asked his mother about Namsamay's whereabouts, she would lie, sending him in another direction. This continued for a long time. Kesamay began to lose his patience.

Infuriated, he shouted at his mother, 'Mother, enough is enough. I cannot bear your lies any longer. You better tell me where Namsamay is or else I will kill you and eat you up.'

Fearing for her son's life, she quietly went inside the hut and whispered to Namsamay: 'Son, today you better trek down to the valley and then climb a *chungde-ngo yangde-ngo sing*.[1] Also, do not forget to take your bow and arrows to guard yourself from your evil brother. Today I have no option but to tell Kesamay the truth that you are going down the valley. Protect yourself. I wish you good luck.'

Namsamay did as his mother advised him. Kesamay, excited about finally knowing exactly where his brother was, ran to the valley. In his excitement, he forgot to carry his bow and arrows.

Back home, Khappura, knowing that one of her sons would surely die today, sat outside her main door with two plants. The bunch of *ondongphung*[2] to her left was for Kesamay and the one of *seikmari*[3] to her right was for Namsamay. The withering of the flowers would indicate death; if the plant bloomed it would indicate life.

Down in the valley, Namsamay armed with bow and arrows, perched on top of a chungde-ngo yangde-ngo sing awaited his brother. Kesamay reached the valley and seeing his brother on the top of a tree, shouted, 'Finally, I got what I wanted. I have been looking for you for a long time!' Kesamay started to climb the tree. Namsamay, despite several attempts, could not hit his evil brother with an arrow.

Namsamay was left with only one arrow. Kesamay, drawing nearer, roared once again, 'Brother, you have fooled me for many days. You won't be spared this time. I will eat you up.'

All the leaves and branches of the tree shook. Mustering some courage, Namsamay said: 'I made several attempts to save myself from you. Today I have no other option but to surrender before you. There's no escaping now. The only thing I can do is to offer my body to you. You need not attack me. Just look up, close your eyes and keep your mouth wide open. I will jump straight into your mouth.'

Hearing this, Kesamay was overjoyed and closing his eyes opened his mouth as wide as he could. Taking his last arrow, Namsamay aimed it straight into Kesamay's gaping mouth, thus piercing him right through his stomach and in the anus. The evil brother was killed instantly and his huge body came crashing down along one side of the tree, breaking all the branches. This is the reason why the people of the Himalayas, especially the Limboo tribe, believe that this tree does not have any branches on one side. Khappura, seeing the seikmari bloom and the ondongphung wither away, knew Namsamay was alive.

Even after killing his evil brother, the nervous Namsamay remained on top of the tree without eating or drinking for several days. It was only when he saw flies hovering over the corpse, did he climb down. Seeing his brother's body lying on the ground, he broke into tears. 'O dear brother, to save myself from your hands, I have committed a great sin by taking your life. How horrible of me to kill my own brother!' he wept. He vowed to do something to honour his brother's memory.

When he had regained his composure, he began to peel Kesamay's skin and dried it in the sun to preserve it. To satisfy their hunger, Namsamay bartered the skin for salt, garlic, chillies, oil, ginger and other foodstuffs from different places. Unfortunately, the mother-son duo fell ill after eating these items.

When they had been ill for a while, Khappura, as a last resort, approached Tagera Ningwa Phuma[4] and told her about their problem. The goddess immediately sent Phejiri Phedangma[5] to earth to cure and heal them. When he arrived on earth, Phedangma asked Namsamay to call all the *tumyanghangs*, or elderly people, for an assembly to be chaired by Phedangma.

Addressing the gathering Phedangma announced, 'I am compelled to make this announcement because Namsamay had collected those items in exchange of the skin of his own dead brother. Both Khappura and Namsamay must observe fast and mourn for nine days, till the purification rite for the dead Kesamay is conducted. Only then will they be cured of their illnesses.'

Following his instructions, Namsamay and Khappura fasted for nine days till the purification prayers were completed. Since this episode, the practice of mourning for nine days, called *netyakma theem*, became essential in a Limboo family following the death of a family member. In this time, family members abstain from consuming salt, oil, chillies, ginger and garlic.

Once they had recuperated, Khappura reminded Namsamay

of his decision to make something useful as a token of love and remembrance of his brother. Namsamay, as per the Kirat Mundhum,[6] set out for the forest. While walking about in the forest, he thought of looking for a tree on which he could stretch his brother's dried skin and make something useful out of it. The evening sun had begun to fade and Namsamay had not yet found the perfect tree. He had to spend the night in the forest.

When he woke up in the morning, the sun had risen high in the sky. It was an unusual day. Amid the songs of birds and the creaking of crickets, his attention was disturbed by a peculiar sound. He looked around. It seemed to be coming from a hollow at the bottom of the tree under which he had spent the night. He stared at the huge trunk and the leaves. The noise seemed to be that of a swarm of bees humming inside the hollow. On closer observation, he found the tree to be the *hongshing*.[7]

An idea struck him, 'If a piece of hollow log of this tree is cut, its bark thinned and both ends closed with the skin I possess, it might produce some kind of sound when struck by hand or a small stick.' He chopped down a branch and brought home a hollow log. He made a hole in it like a beehive. Then he stretched the dried skin tightly on both sides of the hollow log. Namsamay beat on the skin with his palm. It produced a deep sound, like the roaring of a tiger. *Chang-grug-grug* . . . *Chang-grug-grug* . . . *Chang-grug-grug* . . . The entire area echoed with the resounding beat of Namsamay's hand against the stretched skin.

Namsamay had invented a drum in the memory of his brother! So happy was Namsamay that he lifted the log and hung it around his neck. He realised he could produce two kinds of sounds. The right side produced a shrill, sharp sound, while the left side produced a flat note. There was no end to Khappura's happiness as she danced to the rhythm of the music produced by the drum. People started flocking to their home to hear the new, wonderful sound made by this instrument.

Everyone wanted a drum, to learn how to play it. Some of them became professional drummers. The drum came to be called *kay langsamba*, derived from the name Kesamay. Kay also signifies tiger in the Limboo language.[8] The professional drummers came to be called *kaydemba* or drum holders. Kaydembas later became one of the clans of the Limboo tribe.

Wandering around the jungle and from region to region, some of the drummers noticed the actions of animals, birds and insects. Imitating those actions, the drummers eventually created different dance steps or *langs* along with the pounding sound of the drums. Since then, the playing of the drum is often accompanied by *kaylangs*, or dances, which show different actions of animals, birds and insects.[9]

Today the drum is made either of goat-skin or bull-skin and has become one of the most favourite instruments played during any occasion like a marriage or a housewarming ceremony in Sikkim. The hongshing tree still grows in plenty in the region. And the people believe that the leaves of this tree do not need a breeze to sway, but dance gracefully if there is a truly inspired kaydemba nearby.

References

1. Silk cotton tree (*Bombax malabaricum*), a tall tree in the Himalayas.
2. Basil flowers (*Ocimum basilicum*).
3. Wild celery (*Apium graveolen*).
4. As per the Limboo faith of Yuma Samyo, Tagera Ningwa Phuma is the Mother Goddess, the single Almighty.
5. The highest form of Limboo priest or the religious priests of Yuma Samyo.
6. Limboo holy scriptures, literally, the power of great strength. The most important legacy of heritage for the Limboos.

7. Coral tree. Hongshing is the Limboo name. It is called *phaledo* in common Nepali.

8. A tiger is called *kayba* in the Limboo language.

9. Khireiba lang or stag dance, pengwa lang or barking deer dance, tokmay lang or elephant dance, kenda lang or rhinoceros dance, *singvekwa* lang or leaf dance, puyema lang or flycatcher dance, puttukay lang or dove dance, sijowa lang or swallow dance, perewa lang or pigeon dance, ngevonji lang or fish dance, chiraphema lang or butterfly dance, etc.

Acknowledgements

My exploration of the culture, myth and traditions of the ethnic communities of Sikkim began between 1999 and 2003, when I worked at the *Weekend Review*, an English-language weekly. Some of the stories in this book were collected during that period, when I was doing a series called 'Village Spotting'. My gratitude is therefore owed first to P.G. Tenzing, who not only roped me into the realm of *Weekend Review* but also for recommending my name to my editor, Prita Maitra.

I am grateful to my publisher for bringing out my stories in book form and for the initiative taken to preserve the dying folk heritage of Sikkim.

My deepest gratitude to Prita Maitra for the invaluable inspiration I received over emails at every stage. Thank you for being so good, patient and accommodating.

I warmly thank Pankaj Thapa for the stunning sketches that have added life to the stories, and to Sumitra Srinivasan for being such an attentive editor.

Dawa Tshering Lepcha, thank you for listening to some of the stories and providing helpful comments. A special thanks to Padmashri Sonam Tshering Lepcha, for his generosity in answering the smallest of my queries.

I would also like to acknowledge Sonam Gyatso Dokhangbo, for informing me about the tale 'The Cave of the Occult Fairies', and Gompo Dorje, for 'Lapcha Dem' and 'How Humans Were Saved From Demons'.

Thank you, my brother KCG, and your Limboo friends, who told me about the story 'Namsamay and His Magic Drum'.

Finally, my mother and my late father—storehouse of folk tales: if it weren't for you, I wouldn't have grown up listening to stories. I dedicate this book to both of you.